THE SEASIDE MURDER BEFORE CHRISTMAS

SHANNON SYMONDS

ALSO BY SHANNON SYMONDS

Safe House

Finding Hope

By the Sea Cozy Mystery Series:

Murder Takes a Selfie

Murder Makes a Vlog

Murder Has a Ball

Murder Hosts an Event

Murder is Delivered

page5image361959056

ISBN: 978-1-958626-21-4 Library of Congress control number: TBA

Shannonsymondsauthor@gmail.com

Cozymysteriesbythesea.com

Cover design by Shawnda T. Craig

© 2022 Shannon Symonds Edited by Lisa Rector

Final Proof by Tricia Anson

Typeset by Deb Goodman, Author

Printed in the United States of America

To my mother, Beverly Sappenfield.
How eternally grateful I am to you.
You taught me courage and always stood by me
while I took leap after leap of faith.

CONTENTS

1

Santa?

He found me!

They were supposed to be hiding. But eight-year-old Esther didn't want to hide from Santa. Grandma Mable promised her that if she sent Santa a change of address, he would find her and her daddy wouldn't.

There it was. She heard it again. Sleigh bells on the roof of the Victorian fixer-upper her mother and grandmother had just purchased. Then another noise... reindeer prancing? The sound of the ocean was so loud she wasn't sure.

After throwing back the covers, she ran down all three stories of cold wooden stairs. There was no furniture on the first floor, making every footstep echo loudly. But she didn't care. It was Christmas morning.

The one thing they did have in the spacious living room was the tall Christmas tree they had cut themselves in the mountains. It had one string of white lights, and all the ornaments she'd made with notebook paper, crayons, and dental floss. She was eight and knew her works of art were spectacular. Grandma Mable said that hanging them with dental floss was pure genius.

Only one large, wrapped present was under the tree.

Her heart fell. She knew she should be grateful, but a solitary tear escaped her eyes as she tried not to cry.

Grandma Mable told her they were lucky to be alive and to have their new home by the sea. But this house was stupid and empty. Her dad was in jail. She missed him terribly but hated him for making them run away and hide.

Overwhelmed by the realization that nothing would ever be the same, she closed her eyes and dropped to her knees, all alone in the dark morning hours, to pick up the wrapped box with a single red yarn bow. It was heavy. She wanted to shake it, but she couldn't lift it. She sat down and, using both feet, pushed it back under the tree. It didn't make a sound like a game or toy would. It said, "To Esther and Nephi from Blessings."

She wondered if she was naughty and the heavy box was a large lump of coal.

I knew it. Everything is my fault.

Bells jingled outside.

He came back! Maybe he has more presents.

She ran to the large front door, put her ear against it, and heard footsteps crossing the wooden porch. She knew better than to open the door. She wasn't allowed to unless her mother or grandmother was with her.

Baby Mary began crying so loudly upstairs in her mother's bedroom Esther could hear it all the way downstairs.

There it was again. Another sound out on the lawn. Maybe it was like her book, *'Twas the Night Before Christmas.* Was it a clatter? She should ask Grandma what a clatter was. She went to the window, but it was still dark outside.

More footsteps on the stairs. The baby's cries echoed in the empty house. Esther didn't need to turn around to know her mother was coming with noisy Mary, her annoying little sister. Her mother rushed into the living room, frowning and pale. She shook while she rubbed baby Mary's back, trying to soothe her.

"Esther! Get away from the door," her mother hissed.

Grandma Mable and her nine-year-old Uncle Nephi came from the kitchen. She had a baseball bat in her hand.

"No, Grandma!" Esther said and put herself between Grandma Mable and the front door.

"Esther. You need to move," Grandma Mable said.

Then her tears flowed freely. "It's Santa. He forgot the rest of my presents. Don't hurt him!"

Louder knocking at the door startled Esther, who stepped back, looked at the door, and then back to her mother.

The two women—her mother and Grandma Mable—looked at each other while Esther held her breath, crossed her fingers, jumped up and down, and gazed at them with pleading eyes.

Her mother shook her head while she patted Mary's back and swayed like a baby swing. Grandma Mable scowled and shook her head back at her mother. The baby kept wailing.

"Aren't you going to open the door?" Nephi asked.

Her mother deflated, and Grandma Mable shrugged before she went to the door with the baseball bat hidden behind her back.

"Ho ho ho! Merry Christmas!"

It was Santa. There he stood, as big as life, with a jolly belly and a sack of presents.

"I told you! Santa!" Esther clapped her hands with joy.

Grandma Mable stepped back and let him inside.

"Somebody told me that good children just moved to this house. I've been watching you two." He pointed at Esther and then at Nephi.

Her mother gasped. Wide-eyed, she put her trembling hand over her mouth.

"Luckily, your teacher, Miss Robison, told me where to find you! And, ho ho ho, I have some presents for you." He dumped the bag of presents under the tree, and then he went out the door.

Esther stood, frozen. Grandma Mable moved to close the door.

But Santa poked his head back into the room. "Ho ho ho! It wouldn't be Christmas without new bicycles!" Santa wheeled a matching pair of beach cruisers in. One was yellow, and the other was green.

Santa leaned over the yellow bike and came close to Esther's face.

His eyes. She would never forget those eyes. Crystal clear. A shockingly pale color of blue she would never see again. They were so round she could see the entire blue-colored part of his eyes. They turned down at the outside corners in the strangest way.

"Thank you, Santa. I promise to be good forever. Pinky swear," Esther said softly.

Santa pulled a helmet for each of them out of his bag. "Don't forget your helmets! This one is especially for you, little lady." Laughing loudly, he left the house and walked down the stairs with his empty sack. While Esther watched, he got into a red truck and drove away.

Where is his sleigh?

"Grandma Mable, where are his sleigh and reindeer?"

"In the repair shop, sweetie."

Esther scratched her head as she slowly shut the door. She picked up a present and tore at the wrappings. Nephi rang the bell on the handlebars of his bike.

"Stop!" her mother barked. "We need to check those."

Esther handed her mother her gift so she could check to make sure there wasn't a trick in it that could hurt her.

"You can open this one." Grandma Mable pulled the heavy present from under the tree and gave it to them. Esther and Nephi sat down together and ripped off the paper that covered a regular cardboard box.

Nephi opened the box. His shoulders slumped, and he turned his back on the box. "Books. Stupid books."

"Books," Esther said. She loved to read. She took one off the top. The title was *The Little Princess.*

Maybe he didn't know that I was naughty when I made Dad mad and we had to run away, Esther thought.

2

—·—

S ixteen-year-old Esther and Sophie walked side by side across
Necanicum's town square, past their favorite bookstore, and turned
onto a gravel street lined with pine trees. A blue Victorian with a wraparound porch was tucked into the forest on the edge of town. A freshly
painted sign, hanging below its gingerbread eves, read, "Sandy Stories &
Literal Buns, Ramona Brocklehurst, Antiquarian in House."

Snow rarely fell on Necanicum or anywhere on the Oregon Coast. Instead, heavy, gray clouds hung in the air, raining randomly until winter
winds brought in the next storm. This year had been different. They had
just survived a snowstorm that would be remembered by the small town for
years to come as the Thanksgiving Storm. The snow melted on the gravel
road but still clung to the ground underneath the pine trees and in the
shadows.

Esther looked at Sophie, blew on her red hands, and shivered.

Sophie pushed her round, black glasses up her nose and squinted at Esther
with one raised eyebrow. "You're not getting a case of the nerves, are you?
No one could do this job better than us."

"I'm not nervous," Esther whispered. She tucked a brown curl back under her beanie and shrugged. "It's just... Mom told me employers don't want to hire friends."

"Well, they'll want us. We are experienced, dependable, brilliant, and frankly, willing to work for minimum wage."

The squeak of the screen door caught the girl's attention. An older man wearing coveralls stepped out of the house carrying a large red box and set it on the porch swing.

"I know we'd make great employees," Sophie said. "I just think maybe we should stagger our applications. Why don't you go first and when you're done, I'll go in?"

Esther took off her round glasses and put them in her pocket. She looked at Sophie and shook her head. "I just realized we're dressed alike." She suppressed a giggle. Her greenish-brown eyes twinkled over her dimpled cheeks.

Sophie stopped, looked down at her clothes, and felt her black beanie. "Good Gobstoppers. I knew we should have bought different colored jackets."

Esther shrugged. "Black matches everything. Besides, they were cheap."

Sophie wiggled out of her backpack and peeled off her jacket, revealing a red hoodie.

Esther put her hand over her mouth, trying to hide her smile. "You'll freeze."

"Not if we get going." She pulled out her application before shoving her coat inside the pack and zipping it closed. "Look. Either they take us both or they don't get us. We want shifts together so we can do homework when the store is quiet."

"I guess. Well, here goes nothing," Esther said.

They looked at each other and nodded, walking with purpose. The man on the porch paused, holding a string of Christmas icicles. He stared at the girls and watched silently as they walked up the stairs and across the porch.

"Hello," Sophie said.

A bell jingled when Esther opened the heavy front door. Inside, a fire crackled in the fireplace next to a tall Christmas tree decorated with ornaments resembling small books. Vintage bookshelves filled with new books lined the room. The house smelled as if someone was baking gingerbread.

A middle-aged woman looked up from a cash register placed at one end of a long antique buffet. Her smile was infectious. They smiled back. Her platinum blond hair was up in a messy bun with small green and red Christmas bells pinned around it. Her large brown eyes and red lips were in sharp contrast to her pale skin and silver sequined sweater.

The girls walked in unison like a matched set of soldiers to the cash register, and hesitated, glancing at each other.

The woman closed the register. "Ramona Brocklehurst, Sandy Stories owner and antiquarian. How can I help you two young ladies on this fine shopping day? Are you looking for a gift or a great Christmas read?"

"We... um..." Esther put her neatly typed application, and letters of recommendation, and references on the counter. "We'd like to apply for a job." She pointed at Sophie and then back at herself. "We are experienced librarians, having served for three years in Oceanside High's library under Ms. Cynommon Priest. We have a letter of recommendation. We know the Dewey Decimal System and recently learned to work with a computer to check books in and out and accept fines." Esther finally had to take a breath.

Sophie was staring up at her. Esther opened her mouth to go on when Sophie interrupted. "What she means to say is we believe you would be lucky to have us. We are dedicated, brilliant, and adore books. We know books and therefore will be excellent saleswomen."

Ramona continued smiling. She picked up Esther's application and accepted Sophie's. She looked at the pages and their letters of recommendation while she spoke. "Well, as you can see, we are the new bookstore in town. We don't have a lot of traffic yet, but we do plan to hire a full staff. As an antiquarian, I deal in rare books and often travel. I need a dependable team of people I can absolutely count on to show up on time, work hard, and revere the rare books section."

She looked at the girls and was silent for a moment. Sophie opened her mouth to talk again. Esther grabbed Sophie's hand, hoping Ramona didn't see. Sophie looked up at Esther and closed her mouth.

"I see Ms. Priest has given you both very high recommendations. I will follow up on her letter. You'll be required to learn the inventory, to take orders, and to do some very complicated things. In fact, you must be willing to keep the store secure in my absence and follow strict instructions when working with our rare books. In addition, you will not be able to share what rare books we carry or their value with the general public."

Both girls nodded rapidly.

"Now, let me ask you a few questions." She folded her arms and tipped her head, squinting at the girls. "A customer comes in and wants the number one bestseller on The New York Times list. How do you know which book to show the customer?"

"That's easy." Sophie pulled out her phone and held it up. "We keep track of The New York Times list and can always find it here. We love reading the bestsellers."

Ramona nodded and smiled. "Okay, then. A thirteen-year-old girl comes in with her grandmother, who wants to spoil her rotten. What books would you show her?"

Esther raised her hand as if she was in school and then quickly put it down, embarrassed. "I would show them the illustrated Harry Potter boxed set and the matching Diagon Alley three-dimensional puzzle." Esther pulled her round glasses out of her pocket and put them back on.

"Excellent choice. Are you okay if I schedule you on different days so you aren't distracted?"

"No," Sophie said. "Not at all. Our schedules are very tight, and we study together every chance we get. We intend to be accepted into an Ivy League university and to receive multiple scholarships. If you schedule us separately, our time off will also be separate, and we will get behind in our AP studies."

Esther grimaced and held her breath, waiting while Ramona looked back and forth between them.

"Very well," Ramona said. "But if it doesn't work, one of you will be let go. I will confirm your reference by contacting Ms. Priest. Unless you hear otherwise, come to the store on Saturday morning at nine a.m. I will do a quick employee orientation and introduce you to the person who has leased and will run the Literal Buns coffee shop and bakery."

"Thank you for allowing us to work for you, Miss Brocklehurst," Esther said.

"Ramona. Call me Ramona. I trust your phone numbers are on your beautiful resumes. I will contact you if there is any problem with your reference."

"Thank you. We won't let you down. We will be your best employees," Sophie said.

They walked briskly out of the store and just far enough down the gravel road that Ramona wouldn't be able to hear them before they squealed and held a small celebration.

When they finished jumping up and down and high fiving each other, Esther realized the man hanging Christmas lights was staring. She stopped Sophie and gestured with her eyes toward the slack-jawed man. With suppressed giggles, they scurried back to Main Street.

Saturday morning, the beeping sound of a truck backing up woke Esther from a deep sleep. Sophie, who was sleeping over for the weekend, sat up and squinted at the third-floor window in the James family's Victorian home.

Both girls reached for their glasses and put them on, as they had a thousand times before, and went to the window to see who was on their dead-end gravel road. Esther could see the ocean and blue skies beyond the trees, but those same trees were hiding the noise that had roused them.

"There. Do you see it? It looks like a big truck," Esther said. "It's the Scott's house. It must have sold. I wonder if that's a moving truck."

"Or someone knows the house has been empty and is robbing Mr. Scott," Sophie said.

They looked at each other, locked eyes, and a smile grew in the corner of Sophie's mouth.

"Let's go see," Esther said.

Barefoot, they padded quietly past her mother's room and took all three stories of stairs at a dead run. The sound of their feet broke the early morning quiet and woke Nephi, who had fallen asleep on the couch binge-watching an entire series on television.

Esther motioned for Sophie to come to the living room window. She could see the source of the noise through the sheer curtains.

Nephi joined them and yawned. "What are we looking at?"

"It's a moving truck," Sophie said.

"How do you know?" Nephi asked.

"The sign on the side that says U-Haul," Esther said.

"So. It doesn't mean they're moving in. Wait. Maybe they'll have daughters, lots of daughters." Nephi grinned, his brown eyes sparkling while he wiggled his brows. Sophie took a playful swipe at his muscular arm.

"That little cabin is way too small for more than half a girl," Sophie said.

"Then you'd fit right in." Nephi laughed at his own joke.

"Look." Esther pointed across the street at the small, shingled cabin nestled in twisted Pacific pine trees. "There's someone getting out of the truck."

Sophie's eyes grew wide, and her mouth fell open. "Are you kidding? That man is a truck."

"He isn't that big. I could take him." Nephi chuckled.

"No, you couldn't. Look at the size of his arms," Esther said.

"I can't see what all his tattoos say," Sophie said.

"He has full sleeves. Can you see his face?" Nephi pulled the curtains open and snapped a photo with his cell phone before he closed them.

"Nephi. He'll see us staring at him," Esther said through gritted teeth.

Without answering, Nephi used his fingers to zoom in on the picture he had just taken. Both girls leaned in on either side of him.

"Is that a tear tattooed by his eye?" Sophie asked.

"A prison tattoo..." Esther didn't finish the sentence. She looked up to meet Nephi's angry face with her wide eyes.

A small voice asked, "What are you looking at?"

Esther jumped. "Mary. I didn't hear you come in.

Seven-year-old Mary walked to the window and yanked the curtains open. "Hey, look, a new neighbor." She ran for the door.

Esther stopped Mary by grabbing the back of her nightgown. "You don't go over there until you're with a grownup, Mary."

Simultaneously, Esther and Nephi folded their arms and resumed staring at the massive man with a shaved head as he unloaded furniture from the truck.

An SUV belonging to the Necanicum PD pulled into Esther's driveway and parked. The man across the street stopped with a full moving box in his arms and stared at Esther's stepfather, Joe Hart, or Papa J to Esther.

"Having Papa J for a neighbor might encourage him to move somewhere else," Sophie said.

Papa J took the stairs slowly. He opened the door and caught Mary as she ran to him for a hug. He picked her up, and she squeezed his neck. Smiling at Esther, he put Mary down gently.

"Hey, Mary, why don't you go into the kitchen and find some cereal or something for us to eat for breakfast," Papa J said.

Mary ran to the kitchen. "I get marshmallows in my cereal!"

Esther could tell by the tired look on Papa J's face it had been a rough shift at work. After hanging up his bulletproof duty vest and putting his jacket in the coat closet, he sat on a nearby chair to untie his boots.

"I have some bad news, E." He pulled the first boot off and began untying the second one.

Esther held her breath, anticipating something awful.

"I can tell you," he continued, "because it is already on the local newspaper's social media and there is a press release."

"What happened?" Esther's brows drew together, and she chewed on her bottom lip. She really wanted to bite her fingernails, but Sophie would slap her hands if she did.

"You know Hazel? From Seaside Stories downtown?" Hart asked.
She nodded.

"Of course you do." He pulled the other boot off. "She fell from the second story mezzanine in the bookstore and passed away."

"What?" Esther heard herself say. Anxiety rose from her gut, along with heat and confusion.

"It can't be," Sophie said.

Papa J leaned back against the wall as if it had been a long night. "It was a terrible accident. She was going through a box of old books, quills, and things she bought at a storage unit auction. Raini, you know, Raini Bara, from your class at school? She witnessed it along with a new woman in town."

"Poor Raini!"

"She was a mess. Her mom let that reporter, Abbot, from the Coho County Newspaper interview her." He shook his head and rubbed the whisker stubble on his chin.

Esther gritted her teeth. "Abbot is so aggressive. I wouldn't let him interview my kids."

"You have kids?" Papa J smiled.

Esther snickered. "Very funny."

Papa J rubbed his foot and sat silently for a moment. Leaning forward, he said, "Raini said Hazel was excited about something in the box, but we all looked through it and we're clueless. I couldn't figure out why old books, a quill, and dusty bottles of ink would be exciting. Raini said Hazel called down to them and said, 'Look!' She held up an old copy of *Pride and Prejudice* and leaned on the railing over the cash register on the first floor. The railing was loose, and it gave way."

Esther folded her arms and frowned. "Someone made a mistake. That doesn't make sense. If the railing was rotten, she would have fixed it. She and her partner, Jack, love that store. Something's wrong."

Nephi smirked and buddy-punched Esther's arm. "Not everything is a murder."

"You've said that before, and we're always right," Sophie pointed at his face from her four-foot-eleven frame.

"Guys," Hart said. "Give Hazel some respect, okay?"

Esther felt a knot where her heart should be. "I loved Hazel. Her southern accent made everything she said somehow funnier."

"A lot of people loved her." Hart grunted as he stood and gave Esther a hug.

"What will happen to the bookstore?" Esther asked.

"Jack told me he was going to close it. I hope he changes his mind. I guess he has family in Arizona and misses the sun."

"I wondered how a town this small could sustain two bookstores. Now I guess Sandy Stories doesn't have any competition." Sophie looked at Esther and shrugged.

Papa J stretched slowly. "What's for breakfast?"

"Bacon, if you give me money for the store," Nephi said.

"Bacon it is." He pulled cash out of his wallet and gave it to Nephi. "Girls, let's make some banana pancakes to go with the bacon."

Just as Papa J went into the kitchen, Esther's mother came down the stairs, yawning and pushing the pile of curls on her head out of her eyes. "What's going on?"

"Nephi's going for bacon," Sophie said.

Esther's mother smiled. "Yum."

Esther followed her mother into the kitchen, where Grandma Mable already had pancakes on the griddle. "Papa J was telling us about Hazel."

"I heard," Esther's mother said. "It was on the scanner group on social media. So sad."

Esther took the orange juice out of the refrigerator and looked at Grandma Mable. "We have a new neighbor."

"So I see." Grandma Mable put the first pancake on a plate. "I heard you talking about him."

Esther's eyes narrowed, her brows furrowed, and she tilted her head. "Did you see him? He has a prison tattoo."

"So does your father. I thought by now you kids had learned something about judging others." Grandma Mable sighed. She shook her head. "There's only one way to find out who he is."

Grandma Mable left the kitchen, heading to the front door.

Sophie spun around, her mouth open, and she gasped. "She's going over there!"

"No!" Esther jumped up, and they ran to the living room. It was too late. Grandma Mable was gone. They went to the window and saw Esther's redheaded grandmother marching with purpose toward the neighbor, who was holding a white pile of fluff that barked at her.

"Shush, Cookie." The man held the dog close and stroked it.

"Cookie?" Esther bit her lip to keep from laughing.

Mable crossed his lawn, holding out her hand for Cookie and smiling. Cookie licked her, obviously approving of her syrupy fingers. Mable walked with the neighbor toward the front door of the little cabin.

"Biscuits," Sophie said. "Now we can't hear what they're saying. I'm starving. Let's find some whipped cream for the pancakes."

3

E sther picked up her breakfast plate and carried it to the sink. "You're going to love the new bookstore, Mom. You guys should go see it today. When you walk in, you're surrounded by books and the smell of gingerbread."

"Should we be worried?" Sophie asked.

"About what?" Nephi asked. His mouth was full. He washed his food down with orange juice.

"You're right. Shouldn't Grandma Mable be back by now? What if something happened to her?" Esther asked.

"To her?" Esther's mother chuckled, and so did Nephi and her stepfather. "He's the one I'm worried about. If she sees any reason that he's... Well, let's just say she can take care of herself."

Esther knew it was true. Her grandmother was a force to be reckoned with.

Papa J's phone rang.

"Oh, no. You were out all night. Tell me that's not work," Esther's mother said.

He looked at his cell. "No. I left the new rookie, Anderson, in charge. Nobody go anywhere. Just a second. Hello?" He walked out of the kitchen.

Sophie crossed her eyes at Esther, who shrugged. "What's that—?"

Sophie didn't get a chance to finish her sentence. Papa J came back into the kitchen, smiling, and hugged her mother.

"Who wants to go Christmas shopping?" Papa J asked.

Her mother moaned. "Okay, but we will have to take your car, and it's in worse shape than mine. I love Christmas, but there's snow on the mountain between here and Portland. My four-wheel drive needs new tires."

Papa J scooped Esther's mother up.

"Put me down!" Her mother protested, but she was smiling.

"Gross," Sophie said. Esther laughed with Nephi. Mary was squealing and jumping up and down. They followed Papa J to the door and out onto the front porch.

Esther's mother's mouth fell open as Papa J set her down barefoot on the cold wood. "I don't..."

Her mother looked up at Papa J, who wrapped her in a tight embrace, kissed her, and said, "Merry Christmas."

Grandma Mable turned off a brand-new black Jeep Rubicon she had parked in front of the house. It had a giant red ribbon on top. Grandma smiled, held up her cell, and began snapping photos of Esther's mother in her robe.

Esther's mother ran barefoot down the steps, across the wet lawn, and to the Jeep. "It can't be. How did you...?"

Grandma Mable shook her head. "Grace. Don't ruin this moment with a budget conversation." She smiled and held out the car fob.

Esther's mother put her hand over her mouth as she opened the driver's door. She looked back at Papa J and openly wept. "No one has ever been this sweet." She let go of the door and ran back to Papa J and hugged him, joyfully sobbing.

"Hey now, none of that. This is all I'm giving you this year. I promise to be Ebenezer when I fill your stocking." He laughed. "Who wants to go Christmas shopping?"

"Me! Me! Me!" Mary exclaimed.

"Okay. Get dressed. What about the rest of you? We can take two more."

"I don't suppose you can wait until noon?" Esther asked. "We have our new employee orientation." She shrugged.

"That's great!" Papa J said. "Because you will have to pay half of the car insurance on the Cherokee."

Esther's heart dropped into her stomach. "I can't drive."

"You can! We passed the written and the driving test. I know you can. You've got this," Sophie said. "We've got a car!"

"Sweetie," her mother was looking at Papa J, her brows raised, making the mom face Esther was so familiar with. "Maybe we should discuss this first."

Papa J bit his lip. "Right. Like your mother said."

"Grace," was all Grandma Mable had to say. She folded her arms, and her mother slowly smiled.

"Oh, alright," Esther's mother said.

Sophie squealed, arms in the air. Esther didn't know if she should panic or celebrate, so she made a face at Sophie and high-fived her. Esther was happy and terrified all at the same time.

"Okay, Mary, Mom? Are you coming? Let's get dressed." Her mother clapped, and just like that, Esther was happy again. "Esther, are you sure you can't come?"

Esther shook her head and twisted one of her brown curls around her finger.

"What is it, Esther? What?" Her mother asked.

"It's tradition to cut a Christmas tree together this weekend," Esther said. "This is Papa J's first Christmas with our family." She glanced up at him and back to her mother. "It's a tradition." She held her breath and waited for his answer. She didn't know why, but she couldn't stand the thought of missing out on getting a tree the weekend after Thanksgiving.

"I think that sounds wonderful. What time will you be home from your orientation?" Papa J asked.

"Around noon."

"We will be back to pick you both up if it's okay with Sophie's parents." Papa J hugged her. His random displays of affection always surprised Esther. She was still learning to navigate her relationship with her stepfather, and a household where men were touchy feely all the time instead of angry and to be feared.

Sophie hugged them both. "This is the best day of my life. A friend with a car!"

Mary joined the group hug.

"Shotgun!" Papa J shouted. They scattered as he and her mother raced for the house to get ready, laughing, with Mary and Grandma Mable following.

4

E sther and Sophie closed the front door, crossed the large porch, and stood at the top of the steps looking at Hart's old, white 1996 Jeep Cherokee.

"Do you have the keys?" Sophie asked.

Esther nodded but didn't move.

"Your stepdad rocks. I can't imagine my dad buying my mom or me a car for Christmas. He never does anything unpredictable. The best gift he ever gave me was my laptop, and that blew my mind until I got the lecture about using it for my college applications and only for important things like schoolwork."

"My dad didn't give me a car either," Esther said.

Sophie didn't respond. The conversation had clearly shifted. Esther was eight hundred miles away, imagining Christmas in a Utah prison. She wondered what Christmas would be like for her bio-dad, who was in prison for trying to kill her mother when she was pregnant with Mary, and then later attempting to kidnap Esther, along with a long list of other crimes.

"I got another letter," Esther said.

"I thought you were doing video calls now."

"We are. This was written by the prison therapist, I guess. It seems it's time for him to make amends. She wanted to know if it was okay for him to send a Christmas gift and a letter of accountability."

"Crepes," Sophie said softly. "What did you tell them?"

Esther took a deep breath and let it out slowly. "I haven't yet. It came in the mail yesterday. But I did decide something."

"What's that?"

"After I saw him on video, his scarred face, missing fingers, and the damage from the shootout on that boat, I realized he wasn't the monster of my nightmares."

"Really?"

"Yes." Esther was silent for a moment. Still looking across the lawn at the Jeep, she said, "All I saw on the screen was a sad man, beaten up, and I pitied him. Stupid, huh? A criminal, an abuser, and all I could think was how sorry I felt for him."

"I don't feel sorry for him. He got what he deserved. He should be in for life, not in some minimum-security mindfulness camp for criminal masterminds," Sophie said. "Seriously. I don't know how you can forgive him."

"Mom was right. When I did forgive him, it wasn't for him. It was for me. And then suddenly, all I felt was pity. I feel sorry for him, really."

"What are you going to do?"

"He can send me what he wants. I am making something to send to him."

"Can I see it?" Sophie asked.

"Maybe when I'm done with it. I might still change my mind and throw the whole thing away." Esther looked at Sophie, smiled and shrugged, trying to look as if it didn't matter that she was as sad as if her world had been obliterated. Which it had, by the man she had just forgiven.

Taking a deep breath, Sophie squinted at Esther and, pointing her finger, quietly said, "Esther James, how long are you going to let Morgan David Day, your dad, have control of your life and take away all your joy? Every single second that you wallow in your past and let it change the course of your future, you are letting him control you. Look around!" Sophie waved her hands around. "He isn't even here. He's in prison. Not only that, he's in a comfy, touchy-feely prison. Meanwhile, you are giving him permission to taint every single day of your life with fear."

Stepping back, Esther gasped, her eyes scanning the yard. Her hand covered her mouth, but she didn't speak.

"Look! Crepes. You have everything. You have a father, okay, a stepfather, who loves you so much he just handed you his car! Okay, so you have to drive and insure it. Seriously, Esther. Your family rocks, and your boyfriend is hot. If you don't stop being such a negative Nellie, you're going to miss all the fun." Sophie put her hands on her hips and frowned.

Now Esther had both hands over her mouth. A snort escaped between her fingers, and then she parted her hands to reveal a smile. While laughing, she said, "Sophie Ito, I love you. Don't ever stop telling me the truth."

"Well, don't wait for me to apologize." Sophie folded her arms, but her stern look fell apart.

"No one can wait long enough for you to apologize! We'll all be dead and long gone before that happens." Esther shook her head.

"There you are. Back to death. Just do me a favor. Let people love you. Feel the joy, would you?" Sophie smiled and let Esther give her a sideways buddy hug.

"Got it. Let the fun begin," Esther said.

"Deal. Besides, we better go. We don't want to be late on our first day," Sophie said.

Light snow began falling as they crossed the lawn and got into the Jeep. Sophie rolled down her window, leaned out, and tried to catch a snowflake on her tongue. Esther laughed, and just like that, she felt the weight lifting, gone and forgotten. *He isn't going to ruin another day*, she promised herself.

"Let's do this thing," Sophie said. They knuckle-bumped each other.

Hands at ten and two. Holding her breath, Esther closed her eyes and turned the key.

"It's better to drive with your eyes opened." Sophie snickered.

Esther opened her eyes and put the old Jeep Cherokee in drive.

"Now, take your foot off the brake." Sophie's laugh was contagious.

Esther kept her foot on the brake. "Stop!"

But neither of them could quit laughing. Esther snorted. The nervous laughter got worse. The dam broke, releasing all the pent-up tension in uncontrollable giggles. Finally, she held up a hand in Sophie's direction, signaling her surrender. After another minute, she wiped the tears from her eyes, took her foot off the brake, and eased onto the road.

"Biscuits. I forgot to signal."

"Pretty sure you're okay on this busy road." Sophie was being sarcastic. The road was completely empty, but Esther noticed Sophie also locked her door and tugged on her seat belt to make sure it was securely latched.

Gradually, she picked up her speed to ten miles per hour and eased onto the old bridge crossing the Necanicum River. The stop sign was coming.

She turned on her signal and smiled to herself. It was a four-way stop, and no one was in sight.

Hand over hand, she turned the wheel to the right and followed the small-town road south. She was doing it. She rolled down her window and was feeling relaxed when there was a loud honk. She jumped, her heart beating, and looked in the rearview mirror just in time to see a large truck pull around her and pass her, speeding down the quiet, cottage-lined street.

Sophie hung out the passenger window, shaking her fist. "Hey! Rude!"

"Sophie! There are road-rage laws."

"How did passing us benefit him? He'll just get to where he is going a whole thirty seconds ahead of us."

Esther's eyes grew the size of saucers when she realized the truck was stopped at a red light and she would have to stop right behind it. She sunk down in her seat and rolled her window up.

"Crepes. Lock your door," Sophie said. The nervous giggling started all over again.

"Driving is dangerous."

The truck turned left, and Esther turned right, past a man sitting on the corner with a dog wearing a Santa hat and a sign that read, "Any help please." If the man wasn't enough to break her heart, the dog was more than enough. *Where was he when it was snowing?*

Two blocks down and three minutes after leaving her home, she turned left and parked in front of the Sandy Stories bookstore and felt her whole body relax as she got out and locked the car door.

"Where are the keys to the Jeep?" Sophie asked.

"Oh, no!" Esther closed her eyes and gritted her teeth. "In the ignition."

"Hm. No worries. I left my window down anyway." Sophie reached inside the Jeep and retrieved the keys.

The Christmas lights and tree in the bookstore window looked inviting in the gray winter weather. The happy bell on the door tinkled, and Ramona welcomed the girls with a broad smile.

"We're gathering by the fireplace," Ramona said. She pointed toward a circle of chairs. Ramona sat in a leather wingback chair closest to the fireplace. Raini, who had worked at the Seaside Bookstore and was with Hazel when she died, was sitting next to Ramona on a matching leather ottoman. Clearly, Raini had been crying. Her nose and pale blue eyes were red. After blowing her nose with a well-used tissue, she looked through Esther and Sophie, and then looked at her feet, hiding her face in her light blond hair.

Esther didn't recognize the middle-aged woman who sat next to Raini. She smacked her gum as loudly as she dressed. Leather pants pinched at her middle while red heels and a red sweater with sequined poinsettias completed the look.

The hair raised on the back of Esther's neck when she saw Kol Diavalo, senior at Oceanside High, leaning back in his chair, arms folded, long legs stretched out. Sullen as always, he was dressed in black from head to toe except for his jeans. On anyone else, the look would have said he was trying too hard, but Kol made black look good. He glowered at her, with his brown eyes partially hidden by his thick, black hair.

On the other side of the fire, the older gentleman in the same jumpsuit was sitting in a leather wingback that matched Ramona's. A black cat was curled up in his lap, purring, telling Esther that he had the stamp of approval from a cat, making her smile. He was middleweight but had his hands resting on a little belly. He had gray hair on his head, hands, and in his ears and nose. *And yet, he looks kind of sweet, innocent,* she thought.

Esther and Sophie took off their coats and sat next to the sleeping man. He snorted and woke, sat up, and unfolded his arms.

Ramona smiled. "Girls, I believe you know Raini and Kol from school. This is Alvah Sable." Ramona gestured to the woman with the red heels. "She worked at the bookstore with Raini."

Alvah blew her nose loudly, but Esther noticed she didn't shed any tears. Raini, on the other hand, was a fountain of salty sadness.

"And this is my brother, Stanley Brocklehurst. You can call him Stan." Ramona indicated the man who had been sleeping. The man nodded, gave them a simple smile, but never spoke.

"Well, this is our Christmas crew, except for our part-time help. The school librarian, Cynommon Priest; and my sister, the new high school principal, Miss Brocklehurst; will assist us when needed or for events."

"Biscuits. The principal?" Sophie whispered.

Esther opened her eyes wide and nodded in agreement. Ramona looked down her nose at Sophie with one eyebrow raised. Surprised, Esther was sure Ramona was suppressing a smile. She bit her lip and then cleared her throat.

She probably knows her sister should be riding a bicycle and chasing Dorothy to Oz, Esther thought.

Ramona's sister, Desdemona Brocklehurst, like Kol, only wore one color, black. Esther thought it matched her soul and permanent mood. She was like the Dark Lord, always watching and waiting for you to give her a reason to haul you in and humiliate you by calling your parents.

The front door opened, making the shop bells tinkle. Esther gasped, her hand over her mouth. Their new neighbor stood by the front desk. Esther was sure he was well over six feet tall and built like a brick wall, with muscular jaws on his bald head. Studying the group, he frowned with his entire face, making his neck muscles bulge.

Ramona stood. "Meet Ash Corradao. He is the owner and manager of Literal Buns."

"I'm here for the key," Ash said.

"Biscuits," Sophie whispered.

5

— • —

E sther parked the Cherokee with one wheel on the lawn.

"Wait. I'll guide you." Sophie got out and went in front of the SUV and directed Esther like an aircraft marshaller with their orange batons at the airport. "Back. Right. Crank it left."

Once parked correctly, Esther got out and put the key in her pocket before locking the driver's side door. "Sophie, your window is still down."

"This is Necanicum. Pretty sure it's safe," Sophie said.

The front door to her house opened, and Parker, Esther's boyfriend, jogged down the stairs, smiling.

"He's too perfect," Esther said. The sun made his blond hair shine, and she was sure his teeth were sparkling.

"Negative Nellie," Sophie said.

Parker hugged both girls and kissed Esther's cheek. In his perfect British accent, he said, "Nephi called, and Papa J said Paisley and I can tag along. I have the van, and I'm ready for a real American Christmas tree.

The family, including Parker's twin, Paisley, poured out of the house.

"Who's riding with us in the magic machine?" her mother asked.

"Me!" Mary climbed into the new Jeep. Grandma Mable and Papa J joined Mary.

"Let's take the van. Unless you want to drive your new car. Do you love it?" Parker beamed.

"I don't know..."

Sophie poked Esther with a pointy elbow.

"I love it! We are finding the joy today," Esther said. Sophie nodded her approval, and Esther laughed.

Parker held the passenger door to his classic VW Van open for Esther. Nephi, Paisley, and Sophie piled into the back. The engine rattled to life, and they followed Esther's mother onto the road, across the bridge, and down Highway 101.

"Where are we going?" Parker asked.

Esther smiled. "Our favorite Christmas tree farm. It's up by Saddle Mountain."

The little caravan left Highway 101 and turned onto the Sunset Highway. Ten miles and ten minutes later, they turned off the main road. The snow was coming down heavier in the mountains. The road had a skiff of white that made Esther's heart pick up the pace. It rarely snowed on the coast, but it often snowed in the mountains.

"Be careful." Her fingers gripped the handle on the dash.

"Don't worry. I've got this." Parker turned and winked at her. Esther tried to wink back, but she was completely incapable of winking. She blinked several times and blushed.

Just then, the van slid.

"Biscuits!" Sophie yelled while everyone else screamed, including Parker, until the van came to a stop.

He smiled sheepishly, put it back into gear, and continued crawling along at a slower speed.

Esther's phone rang.

"Yes," she said. "No. We're fine. Okay. I'll tell him. Papa J says you're doing great. Keep our seatbelts on and slow down."

Parker nodded but didn't take his eyes off the road. Miles into the forest, the trees blocked the winter sun, and they gingerly drove over patches of ice. Then the trees opened to a snow-covered field filled with more than fifty elk, including a massive seven-point bull whose head was level with Esther's. They stopped grazing on the grass that rose above the snow and looked at the van, chewing. Parker slowed to a stop.

"Aren't they beautiful?" Esther asked.

"Amazing." Parker said. The bull bugled and began walking toward them. He put himself between them and the herd.

"And dangerous, dude. Let's go," Nephi said.

Parker put the van back in gear and followed the road higher and higher. The Jeep pulled off the road and looked like it disappeared in the trees. The van followed, turning onto a rough gravel road.

"Sorry! The suspension is a little bouncy," Parker said.

The trees were so tight and the ferns that grew below them were so thick there was no place to turn around. After a few minutes, they emerged in a gravel parking lot. A dozen cars were parked in front of a large blue-and-white farmhouse, which was decorated for Christmas. A small red barn's doors were open. You could see fire in a barrel inside. People talked and gathered, sipping hot cider and shopping in the small gift shop filled with local-made art and ornaments.

Esther pulled her beanie on and wished she had gloves. Parker opened her door. His breath made clouds in the cold air.

Esther's family was parked and trying to catch up with Mary, who was running toward the barn.

"Let's get a saw," Esther said.

"I can't believe this place," Paisley exclaimed. "It's gorgeous. We must bring Mum and Dad back. Oh! And we need to bring Madison and Bridget."

Parker and Paisley's parents, the Stuarts, had moved from Britain earlier in the year and purchased the Captain's Cove Mansion in Necanicum. Their friend and world-famous, bestselling author, Madison Merriweather, and her daughter, Bridget, had followed them, and bought a small home a few blocks away from the Stuarts.

Near the door to the barn, Parker picked a saw out of a wooden barrel and looked at the blade. "Mum said we could get the tree for the study. It needs to be ten or more feet tall."

"No problem." Esther grinned. "There are a few trees here."

They walked around the barn into seven acres of Christmas trees of various heights and sizes. Douglas firs with soft branches and noble firs with strong branches and prickly pine needles were dusted with snow.

Esther couldn't help it. She pulled her phone out and snuck a photo of Parker's awestruck face as they wandered away from the others.

"What do you think of this one?" he asked.

"It's a Douglas fir. How heavy are your ornaments? The branches aren't very strong," she said.

A slow smile spread across his face. "I take it you're not a fan?"

She laughed. "I like noble firs. They're strong and can carry a lot of weight."

"Just like me?" He flexed his biceps and gave her a goofy grin, cheeks bright red from the cold.

He's beautiful, she thought. *Embrace the joy.* She hugged him. *Sophie's right.* He held her, hot breath blowing on her cold neck.

"Hey! Break it up, you two," Nephi said.

Esther looked up, and he hit her right in the shoulder with a snowball.

"Nephi!" Esther made her own snowball.

Suddenly, it was complete mayhem. Papa J helped Mary throw snowballs at her mother; Parker chased Nephi. Paisley threw snowballs at Parker.

When the chaos died down, Esther realized she didn't see Sophie.

"Parker? Have you seen Sophie and Grandma Mable?" Esther asked. The trees were thick enough that anyone more than five feet away from her would be swallowed up and lost in them. She wasn't sure which way the barn was. There weren't any landmarks. Her heart began to race again.

She closed her eyes. *No. Breathe.* She opened them, and cupping her hands around her mouth, she called, "Caw-caw! Caw-caw!"

Parker's eyes drew together, and one of his brows raised, questioning.

She called one more time. "Caw-caw! Caw-caw!" She motioned for him to be quiet.

Then she heard it. "Caw-caw! Caw-caw!"

Parker laughed loud and long.

"Come on," she told Parker. The group followed her as she continued to call, "Caw-caw! Caw-caw!" And the answer would echo hers, over and over again, until she and Sophie found each other.

"Where did you go?" Esther asked.

"Only to the best tree on the farm. I've been guarding it," Sophie said.

"It's magnificent!" Paisley said.

34

"Your turn to saw, bro," Nephi said.

The trees were tied to the tops of the cars, and the tired group sipped cider as they rolled down the mountain. The radio played Christmas music softly. Nephi and Sophie were in a heated debate about the names of Santa's reindeer.

"I heard about Hazel. I know how much you liked her. I am so sorry," Parker said.

"We met there. You and me. I mean, that's the first time we really talked," Esther said.

He looked at her for a moment. He was blushing. "I remember."

"I loved the bookstore. I know you will probably be like Nephi and think I see murder everywhere, but seriously, I don't think it was an accident. That store was in perfect order."

"It seemed like it. I didn't hear much, just what was on the scanner page on social media and the short article in the local online news. Something about her finding something in a box. Abbot inferred that she wasn't paying attention. It's like he blamed her. Honestly, Hazel deserved more than two paragraphs." Parker shook his head.

"Is that all they gave her? I just keep wondering what was in the box that was so special, or about the book she was looking at, before she fell. Whatever it was, it had her complete attention. I wish I could go in and look through it. A police officer may not recognize something a book fan like me and Sophie might see."

"I don't think you think everything is a murder. You are seriously brilliant when it comes to putting a puzzle together. You see the world differently," Parker said.

"Through the lens of mistrust. I know. I'm working on it. I promised Sophie I would find my joy. I'm going to have to shop the self-help section at Sandy Stories."

"I forgot to ask. How was your first day? Do you like the store owner?" Parker asked.

"Ramona? I do. But did I tell you about our new neighbor?"

"No."

"He owns the Literal Buns coffee shop and bakery attached to the bookstore," Esther said. "He moved in today across the street in Scott's old cabin. He's huge, and he has a prison tattoo. You know, the tear by the eye?"

"A teardrop?"

"It's a prison thing. It can be about gangs or mean you killed someone. Anyway, he has this cute dog, but he has a lot of tattoos and shaves his head. He looks scary."

"Mable wasn't afraid." Sophie leaned forward between Parker and Esther. "Did you find out what they talked about?"

"The tree farm was the first chance we had to ask, and I totally forgot," Esther said.

"Yeah, we saw. You were occupied." She gave Esther a cheesy grin and wiggled her eyebrows.

"Watch it, short stuff. We'll make you sit on top of our tree and try to be an angel," Nephi said.

A new song played on the radio. "*You know Dasher and Dancer...*"

"Turn it up!" Sophie yelled. "I want to show Sasquatch here that he's wrong about the reindeer names."

6

The James home was a three-story Queen Anne with a round turret. Esther's desk sat under a window in the turret. She wrestled the wooden window open and put a dog-eared Webster's Dictionary on the sill to hold it open. She loved the fresh sea air, the sound of seagulls, and even the smell of salty fish. It was the smell of home.

School was out, and the sky was crystal clear when she wrapped herself in a mint green afghan that her Grandma Mable had crocheted for her and opened her laptop to join a video call with her father in prison.

She logged into the prison's visiting system.

Sophie was pretending to read her AP History textbook on Esther's bed as if she wasn't listening in, but Esther knew she was hanging on every word. Her brilliant friend hadn't turned a page since she opened the book. And she kept checking the time on her phone.

The words, *Waiting for the host to begin the meeting*, and a spinning wheel were on her laptop screen when her Cheshire cat, Miss Molly Brown, leapt softly onto her lap. Esther gathered her up and stroked her warm fur while she purred loudly.

When Esther was a small child, her father had been imprisoned for trying to kill her mother in front of her. The abuse they'd survived still haunted her. He'd been so dangerous; Utah's victim's assistance program had helped them move far away to hide by the sea. Earlier in the year, after working his way up to a model prisoner, her father, Morgan David Day, had walked away from a work release job site.

For years, she had been safe. Esther, her mother, and Mary had moved on and built a life with Grandma Mable, and her mother's brother, her uncle, Nephi. No one in town had known the story until her father returned and made the front page of the local paper. They plastered her whole messy life all over social media.

"We're going to be late for our first actual day at work," Sophie said.

Esther shrugged. "Sorry."

The screen changed, prompting her to answer a series of questions and approve the recording of the meeting. And then there he was.

He always wore the same thing, an orange-and-black-striped romper or jumper. She wasn't sure what it was called. He was always clean-shaven with short wavy hair, a close match to her brown curls but streaked with gray. She looked a lot like her dad, but his face and hands were scarred. He was also missing parts of some of his fingers, a grim reminder of the moment he did something so shocking it changed the trajectory of their relationship.

"Hello? Esther? Sweetheart?"

She grimaced, hating it when he called her that.

It was silent for a moment.

"Hi," was all she could muster.

After his escape from prison, he came to claim her, his child, with the help of a fellow prisoner who hooked him up with sex traffickers to help him hunt her down. Then a strange thing happened.

After a failed kidnapping attempt, he and the traffickers were on a boat at sea. Her mother said that in a fight, he'd tried to protect Hope, one of the trafficker's victims. He shot and killed one of the traffickers, fought with another, fell overboard, and was cut up by the ship's propeller.

Somehow, he survived, and over the course of this year, he'd tried to reestablish a relationship with Esther. After years of abuse, absence, and then uncharacteristic heroism, he'd asked for her forgiveness and said he was working on making amends.

She looked down at Miss Molly, whose eyes were closed.

"Esther?" he asked. Looking up, she saw him run his gnarled hand through his short hair. "Did you get the letter? Can you talk?"

Wanting to change the subject, Esther said, "I got it. We have a new neighbor." She looked down at the cat while she talked. "He's massive, and I think he has a prison tattoo. Grandma went over to talk to him, but we think he's dangerous. What does a tear tattoo by your eye mean?"

It was silent. She looked back at the screen. Her father had the strangest expression. It pulled his scars to one side. She studied it until she realized it was a lopsided frown interrupted by patchwork skin.

Her father closed his eyes and took a deep breath. After he let it out slowly, he said, "Esther Day, you of all people should know not to judge a book by its cover."

Her eyes narrowed, and she almost growled. "That's not my name. My name is Esther James. You have no right to scold me."

His head pulled back. She gasped, realizing tears pooled in his eyes. Immediately, pity washed over her. As fast as her anger was kindled, a single tear put it out. Miss Molly dropped to the floor and left her, as though she were leaving a naughty child, and wasn't she?

"Look," he said. He took one, then two deep breaths, looking down at something off screen. He wiped an eye with the back of his mangled hand. "I know I don't have any rights."

She realized his chest heaved because he was trying not to cry.

"I'm sorry, Dad." She couldn't believe the words as they came out of her mouth.

He shook his head, wiped his eyes again, and said, "It's just that I know what it feels like to be judged."

And then it hit her. She had brought the neighbor up to change the subject, and instead she had revealed the part of her that she hated most, the part that struggled with trust and was always on the lookout for risk, waiting for the other shoe to drop... no... to smack her square in the face.

Tears betrayed her. She was so overcome with shame she wanted to slam the computer shut. She reached out for Miss Molly, but Sophie was the one who responded, squatting close to her, holding her hand, and handing her a T-shirt to wipe her nose on.

"I'm sorry," she said, again. Her voice was ragged and breathy. "I got the letter."

"I know it sounds like a big deal, but I promise I'm ready. I will make it as painless as possible."

It is a big deal, she thought. *Why does he have to do it now, at Christmas?*

"I have to get to work," Esther said.

"You got a job? That's great! Where is it?"

"Just a bookstore. Sophie's waiting. It's our first day." She glanced at Sophie, who was watching like a guard dog.

"Oh. Okay. Um. Can we set a date for our meeting together? Can we do it Christmas Eve?"

She closed her eyes and chewed on her bottom lip. She said, "I have a boyfriend, and we have plans." *It's sort of the truth,* she thought to herself.

"Oh, right. It's just, you see... I'm sending something to the house. Part of it might show up early. What if the gift arrived early, on Christmas Eve? If it's before your work and plans, would it be okay?"

She didn't know what to say.

He was silent, rubbing the back of his neck and looking at her from under knit brows and through pleading eyes. He wiped sweat from his forehead with the sleeve of his jumpsuit.

"Sure."

"Great! That's great. I will try to get it there early and coordinate the arrival with your mother. You won't regret this, sweetie, I promise."

She already regretted it. Miss Molly was back, her soft feet landing on the desk and stepping down into her arms, claws picking at the afghan in her lap.

She squared her shoulders and let out a jagged breath. "Okay. We can talk next week, but I don't want to be late."

"You go. And Esther, I promise, it's a good surprise." He clicked off, and she closed her laptop.

"Says a killer. What kind of 'good surprise' can a killer in prison give you?" Sophie asked.

"I have no idea," Esther said, "but we have to hurry. Bubba asked if we would give him a ride to Literal Buns. He's going to work there as a dishwasher and busboy sort of thing."

She gently placed Miss Molly on her bed and folded the afghan, leaving it in her rocking chair.

Checking herself in the mirror, she crossed her eyes and growled. "This hair."

"Bun it," Sophie said. She handed Esther a scrunchie. Esther quickly made a messy bun, rolled her eyes at her reflection, grabbed the Jeep keys, and ran down the stairs behind Sophie.

The knobby Jeep tires crunched on the tree-lined gravel road to Bubba's house. The girls knew Bubba from school. They became friends when Bubba was mistakenly accused of murder after threatening school violence. It turned out his threat was an ill-conceived attempt to hurt kids he believed hated him. They made peace as they got to know each other.

Bubba lived in Forest Park, a trailer park just off the highway between Esther's house and the bookstore. She watched for broken glass.

They passed their friend Jackson's well-kept trailer, with flowers, vines, and Jackson's original mural, which made it look like it came out of Madison Merriweather's bestselling novel, *Blessed Be*. Following the bumpy gravel drive, past trailers that looked abandoned with broken windows and as if forest moss was consuming them, they took a turn onto the lawn by Bubba's trailer. It was away from the others, which was good. He had nine siblings who could get noisy.

Bubba came running out, followed by his sister carrying Fern, the baby, and the twin girls, who were both crying.

"Don't go, Bubba!"

He bent his six-foot-six frame over and kissed their blond heads. Then he turned and, scowling, ran for the Jeep, ripped the door open, and jumped into the back.

"What took you so long? I could have walked! We're going to be late," he said.

"Why, hello, Bubba. So nice to see you, Bubba," Sophie said. She turned and looked into the back seat, with one eyebrow raised. "Really?"

Bubba buckled his belt and fell back against the seat. "Alright. Just get this rust bucket on the road."

"That's J1G2 to you," Esther said. She patted the dash.

"Seriously? You named your car?" Bubba folded his arms around his lean middle and watched the trees go by out the window.

"Yup. Jeep number one, because I plan to have a new one someday, and G2 for girls two. Because Sophie and I are going to share her."

"The Jeep's a girl now?" Bubba chuckled.

"Of course. Girls rule," Sophie said.

"You're two spoiled girls."

"Hey now. What's wrong with being spoiled?" Sophie asked.

Esther watched Bubba give Sophie what she would call the stink eye. "Don't you want to be successful someday?" He looked out the window. Heat rose from Esther's stomach and to her face. "We're not rich, Bubba. You could be successful too. What's wrong with it?"

"That'll never happen." Flat, expressionless, he shrugged.

Sophie hung over the front seat and used her hands to make a point. "Don't you ever dream? I do. I don't think it matters how much money you have. It's what you do with it that counts, like developing the artificial kidney or solving the wind turbine disposal dilemma. I'm going to an Ivy

League school and will run an international corporation someday. I could hire you to handle cyber security."

"There's no point in dreaming." Bubba's blank look, sloped shoulders, and monotone voice delivered the raw truth. He reminded Esther of a defeated warrior, someone who had lost hope. He leaned his head against the back passenger window and watched the world go by.

Esther thought, *What makes someone give up like that? And why am I embarrassed to have nice things? Do I have hope?*

"My mother says that money is the gateway to freedom and that you have to go after it," Sophie said.

Esther turned to look at Sophie, head tipped, and almost ran them off the road. She jerked the wheel back. "She did?"

Sophie nodded.

"Did you hear about Raini?" Bubba asked.

Esther looked at Bubba's serious face in the rearview mirror.

"Her mom has cancer. Raini doesn't work to pay for dumb stuff. She helps her mom."

"Biscuits," Sophie said. "That's awful. How is her mom?"

His eyes met hers in the mirror for a microsecond. "She has cancer. How do you think she is? Now get us there before we get fired on our first day."

His anxiety was so heavy it filled the Jeep. The gravel road ended, and Esther eased back onto the highway.

Bubba jumped out of the Jeep as soon as it stopped and trotted to the bakery doors where Esther's new neighbor, Ash, waited and followed him in.

The bakery looked different, cleaner, and the trim around the windows was freshly painted, as were the French doors added to the side of a carriage house, an extension of the original home. The trim was cream colored in contrast to the blue house and red doors. A wooden sign over the store read, "Literal Buns." The words were curved like a rainbow around a steaming roll and cup of tea.

Sophie groaned. "That smell. How are we going to work so close to the smell of cinnamon and chocolate without eating all day?"

"Right? At least our shift is only a few hours long," Esther said.

"I think Bubba likes Raini."

"You think?" Esther snickered.

Alvah was at the desk, talking with a woman and her daughter when the girls came in. Esther noticed Stanley hand Alvah a small poinsettia in a red planter. Alvah smiled at Stanley. *How sweet*, Esther thought.

"Look," Esther whispered. She pointed at Stanley and Alvah.

"It's probably just another store decoration," Sophie said.

"It's still cute," Esther said.

Raini was unboxing Christmas books with Ramona, who knelt on the floor, placing them on a low display shelf near the tree. Esther was surprised at how many customers were in the store.

"Oh good. You're here. Raini, I'll see you tomorrow. You did a great job. Do you need to call someone for a ride? It looks like it's started to rain buckets," Ramona said.

"Kol is taking me. He's buying us a cinnamon roll. I'll meet him at the bakery." Raini smiled.

"That sounds delicious," Ramona said, smiling back at Raini.

Esther scanned Raini's face. She was so tiny and pale, Esther wanted to hug her.

Raini smiled broadly at the girls. "Don't you just love Christmas? Ash made gingerbread."

Sophie groaned again. "I'm going to starve to death. What time does he close?"

Ramona laughed. The sound was infectious. "Don't worry. You get a break and can stock up for your ride home." She stood and brushed invisible dust off her black silk pants. "Girls, I want you to meet my boyfriend, Draven Kane."

Silently, a handsome middle-aged man stood from the chair by the fire, where he had been reading.

"Fiancé," Draven said. He held out his hand, and Esther shook it. It was cold and soft.

Esther was immediately fascinated. He looked as if he had stepped out of a magazine or ad for Nordstrom. His face was rugged, with a close-shaven black beard. His brown eyes twinkled under close-cut curly dark hair with gray streaks. He wore a gray tweed jacket with leather patches on the elbows over jeans and a white shirt.

Then Esther saw his umbrella and knew he wasn't from the coast.

Sophie shook his small, moist hand. Ever transparent, she drew her chin in and wiped her hand on her jeans.

"Where are you from?" Esther asked.

"How did you know he wasn't born and bred in Oregon?" Ramona smiled and shook her head.

Esther pointed at the umbrella hung on his arm. "It's the umbrella. A local would never be caught dead with one. First, a good ocean breeze will turn it inside out. Second, we are proud of our webbed feet and wet hair. We don't let the weather get us down."

"Elementary, my dear Watson," Sophie said.

Draven chuckled, but his laughter didn't rise to his eyes. He was clearly offended. "Liverpool. I'm from Liverpool."

"Oh, Draven. Relax." Ramona patted his arm. "Let's show these girls what you do best. Come on, girls, follow me."

He may be from Liverpool, but his accent and voice sounds like an anchorman from fake Britain, or he's watched too much Downton Abbey, Esther thought.

"He's from Arizona, or that's a spray tan," Sophie whispered, as they followed Ramona.

A new chain hung across the stairway in the entry. Hanging from the chain, a sign read, "Rare books and Request assistance", with an arrow toward the front desk.

"My office is upstairs," Ramona said. The girls followed her up the grand staircase to the second story landing. Double doors were opened on the west side.

Esther could hear her own heartbeat. Books! Not just any books. Her favorite kind—ancient, classic, leather-bound antiquities dripping with history. Never in her life had she seen a more beautiful room. Row after row of books, with a display case near the door holding a rare Geneva Bible that had to be worth thousands.

Another rare book was on a stand and opened to an illustration that took her breath away. She didn't have to look at the title to know that this was *The Lion, The Witch, and the Wardrobe,* by C.S. Lewis. Next to it was a book that made Esther's heart skip a beat with longing. The dust jacket was red, and the title was *Hercule Poirot's Christmas*. A piece of paper stuck out of the book like a marker. When the book had been signed by the author, the bookmark had one word in pencil across the top, signed.

Ramona went ahead of the girls into the room, but Esther was mesmerized by the book.

Draven startled Esther when he asked, "Do you like it? It's a very rare first edition, signed by the author. It's valued at a little over thirty-two thousand."

Esther gasped and looked at Draven. He slowly smiled like a cat who was about to eat a canary.

"That's why I insist every customer be escorted when they come upstairs."

He insists? Esther thought. *Isn't this Ramona's store? Is he a partner?*

"Holy guacamole," Sophie said, eyes round. "Is that real?"

Draven pulled himself up to his full height, towering above Sophie. With one brow raised and through gritted teeth, he said, "Why, of course. I am a member of the Antiquarian Booksellers Association of America, as is Ramona. We collect and treasure rare books. We also hunt them like treasure for anyone that asks. This one already has a home to go to." Then his syrupy sweet smile returned.

"I want to know everything about all the books in this room. Can we learn how an antiquarian works?" Esther asked.

"It's addicting," Ramona said. "Sometimes, late at night, I just must come in, touch the covers, and pinch myself to be sure I'm not dreaming. I love reading in here." She pointed at an antique red velvet and dark wood reading lounge under a large window with a half circle of stained glass above. A wedding ring quilt was folded on the foot of the couch, and a Tiffany lamp decorated a table with a stack of books on it.

Esther scanned the rest of the room. Although windows filled the west wall, they were covered in one-way mirror film, which she guessed protected the books from being damaged by sunlight. The shelving was taller than Draven and lined up like a library.

Stanley came into the room, went to a desk in the corner, and logged onto a computer. Esther noticed a line of ink bottles and a quill laid out on the desk. Curious, she moved closer and realized he was looking at the rare books online.

"Stanley dabbles," Draven said. He rolled his eyes and followed Sophie, who was reaching for a book on the shelf. "Don't touch that. We use gloves when we touch books in this room. And you will never be allowed to handle any of our priceless acquisitions."

Esther's attention returned to Stanley, who was closely examining a quill with small gold reading glasses on.

Stanley didn't seem to notice Esther. While the others moved away, Esther moved behind Stan, who clearly knew what he was doing. The computer was opened to a website with the title, *Bibliotheque,* displaying what looked to Esther like a Medieval Book with beautiful artwork. Fascinated, she stepped closer.

Voices distracted her.

"Draven," Ramona whispered. She was in her office. He joined her and pushed the door closed, but it didn't latch and swung silently open, but only slightly.

"I had it, darling. I wanted to do a little research and authenticate Churchill's signature. It should be on the desk with Stanley," Draven said.

"Did you give Stanley money?" Ramona asked.

Stanley's head popped up, and he looked at the office door, then he looked at her over his shoulder and closed a ledger, which was open on the table. Frowning, he pushed back his chair and passed her, leaving behind the smell of hard work and paint.

Esther noticed there was a small safe tucked under the desk, and naturally curious, wished she could peek inside.

The office door opened, and Draven came out, leaving Ramona watching him, with her brows knit and her arms folded.

Esther went to a shelf and began reading titles.

"Okay, ladies, time to go," Draven said.

Esther jumped. He was standing right behind her. She found Sophie walking among the shelves.

"Sophie, let's go."

"There are some pretty valuable books up here."

Esther glanced over her shoulder to be sure no one was looking. "I know. Check out the safe under the desk. It's probably for the store or maybe for really valuable books. It seems like this room is a place someone, like Kol, could easily break into and steal something."

"I googled the book with the gold leaf art in the display case. You know, the one opened on the stand?"

"Yes." Esther kept her voice low as Draven herded them down the stairs to the store.

When they reached the bottom, Miss Brocklehurst motioned for them to follow her through a dark hallway.

Sophie leaned closer to Esther and whispered. "They aren't priced on regular websites. They are hard to find. I found a Gutenberg Bible for two hundred twenty-five thousand, but I couldn't find a price for a piece like that."

Like a tour guide, Miss Brocklehurst showed them to the kitchen. It had a deep breakfast nook, a long table, and a farm sink. The room was large, white, and bright. Its southern wall was almost all windows, including the French doors leading out to a deck.

"You can leave your lunch or snacks in the refrigerator. I empty it on Fridays, so don't leave your favorite Tupperware behind," Ramona said.

"What's Tupperware?" Sophie asked, making Ramona laugh again. "What? What's so funny?"

"I forget how young you are and how different things are for your generation. Tupperware is a brand name of plastic storage containers.

"Oh. Like Ziploc."

"Precisely." Ramona smiled.

7

— • —

"We've got fifteen minutes left in our shift," Esther said.

"That went fast." Sophie was unboxing bookish Christmas ornaments and using a list to price them.

"Sophie?" Esther whispered.

"Hmm?"

"When we were upstairs, did you see the ink bottles lined up on the desk with an old quill?"

"If I did, I don't remember, which means I didn't," Sophie said. "Why do you ask?"

"Remember, Papa J said that Hazel was looking through a box that had ink, quills, and old books in it. The ink and quills must be valuable. Why else would Ramona and Draven keep a collection on their desk?"

"Decoration?" Sophie shrugged and continued pricing ornaments.

"Draven feels..."

"Creepy," Sophie said, finishing her sentence.

"We should do some investigating and see if the ink or quills are valuable."

The bells on the door tinkled, interrupting their conversation.

"Oy. Can a mate get any service here?"

"Parker!" Esther exclaimed. He gave her a quick hug while they laughed.

"Your Lordship, your accent is distinctly Liverpool," Sophie said.

He gave her a brilliant smile and pulled his gloves off, shoving them into his pocket.

"Did you come to drive us home?" Esther asked. "I have the Jeep, remember?"

"Oh, I remember," Parker said. "In fact, I'm thrilled, but I will be working on some school days. I'm going to miss driving you home from school with our chaperone, Sophie."

"It's okay. I can drive the Jeep," Esther said.

"Rude!" Sophie called from behind the cash register.

He grinned ear to ear. Esther's Uncle Nephi rang the bells and let the door slam, announcing his presence. "Did he tell you? We're going to be working for the new neighbor! Two evenings a week. Bubba is working all the other shifts."

"Does that mean you get a discount on cinnamon rolls and scones?" Sophie asked.

Nephi smiled. "A discount isn't going to help you. No one can bake enough food for you."

Ramona descended the stairs, smiling. "Are the girls helping you? I heard you ask for help when you came in."

Parker's face turned bright red. "No. I was just teasing Esther."

Ramona looked back and forth from Esther to Parker. "Ah. I see."

"I'm sorry, Ma'am. We won't have friends at work," Esther said. "I've been reading various guides to business and successful sales. We really want to do a good job. We won't let it happen again."

Nephi smirked, and Esther gave him the pressed-lip, you-better-not face.

Ramona gave the boys a dazzling smile. "Boys, you are welcome anytime you are purchasing books or moving furniture. You two look big enough to carry a bookshelf with the books still on it. And girls, you've learned enough for one day. You're free to go. Next time you work, I will teach you how to lock up."

"Goodnight, Miss Brocklehurst," Esther said.

"Ramona. I insist." Ramona unlocked the cash drawer and pulled the tray of money out.

"Goodnight, Ramona," Sophie said. "See you soon."

"Let me get our coats." Esther walked quickly to a hall tree in the kitchen and returned with their coats. She held them up so she could see which of the identical coats was smaller.

Nephi tried to help Sophie with her coat. She slapped his hand.

"Hurry. He is waiting to close the bakery for you. We told him you were dying for goodies," Nephi said.

Outside, the winter evening air was chilly, and Esther was grateful for her coat. The rain had stopped, but it had also washed away the snow. The Christmas lights that looked like icicles were beautiful but didn't outshine the full moon or the stars.

A small car pulled up the driveway slowly and drove around the house as they walked the long porch to the stairs near the bakery.

"Isn't that a Prius?" Sophie asked. "I hear they can get over forty miles to the gallon and help save the planet."

"Yeah," Nephi said, "but no one ever said, 'Cool Prius.'"

"I love Priuses. I bet no one ever told you your dented blue truck was cool either." Sophie stuck her tongue out at him, making him laugh.

"Why do you think we took the jobs at the bakery? It's time to upgrade our rides," Nephi said.

"But Parker's VW is absolutely perfect," Esther said.

The Literal Buns bakery porch was only a few steps below the house on the west side. Warm yellow light shone out of the curtainless windows. Inside, a giant man—their new neighbor—was mopping the floor, alone, with the radio playing music from a local indie band.

When the French doors opened, Esther was hit by the fragrance of freshly baked goods, coffee, and something else. She couldn't place it. Then she saw a self-serve Crock-Pot full of spiced cedar, with orange slices and cinnamon sticks floating on the top. The aroma took her back to every Christmas morning with her mother, both before and after the divorce and her father's prison sentence.

"Scones and ice-cream! Look at this!" Sophie had her arms outstretched as if she wanted to hug the glass case full of some of the most beautiful Christmas cookies, cranberry scones, and cinnamon rolls Esther had ever seen.

"Don't put fingerprints on my glass," Bubba called from a kitchen window on the wall behind the counter.

"Your glass?" Sophie laughed.

"Ownership of your work and your company's business is the mark of an excellent employee," Ash said.

Esther was startled by his deep voice. It was smooth and low.

Ash leaned on his mop. "And I quote, 'Whether you are the president of a company or the janitor, the moment you step from independence to interdependence in any capacity, you step into a leadership role. You are in a position of influencing other people.'"

"You've read Covey? You know the *Seven Habits of Highly Effective People?*" Sophie squinted incredulously at Ash.

"I had a lot of time to read in prison," Ash said.

Just at that moment, a creaking sound was followed by one crash after another, ending in a thunderous slam—bang. It was so loud, Esther looked up, expecting the building to fall on her. Then she realized everyone was screaming and running for the door, except Ash.

"Stop!" Ash bellowed. "Don't move!"

"But..." Parker started to say.

"Parker, Nephi. You come with me. That sounded like something blew up. Bubba, turn off the gas and all the appliances. You girls, lock yourselves in your car, and call nine-one-one." Ash ran across the deck and onto the porch. Looking over his shoulder at Esther, he yelled, "Go! Now!"

Esther jumped. Sophie pushed her and they ran for her car.

"Wait!" Sophie screamed. "Why are you letting a convict tell us what to do?"

"I don't know!" Esther bellowed back while dialing nine-one-one.

Before the emergency operator answered her call, the door to the bookstore opened and Principal Brocklehurst yelled, "Help! Help!" She motioned for the girls to follow her and ran back inside.

"Nine-one-one, what's your emergency?"

"We don't know. It sounded like an explosion. Now Principal Brocklehurst is screaming for help. I can hear people yelling."

"Slow down, ma'am."

Esther wanted to throw the phone. "Slow down! Slow down! You slow down!"

"Ma'am. Ma'am. I am trying to help you. What is your emergency? Are you at the school?"

"No! I don't know." She began running for the door. "We are at Sandy Stories, the new bookstore."

"I am sending an officer now."

"Send the fire department, send the medics, send the ever-loving mayor! Send Papa J!" Esther shoved her phone into her pocket and followed Sophie up the stairs, who was taking them two at a time. They could hear yelling and noise coming from the rare books room.

She hit the doorframe and froze. All the bookshelves had toppled like a bizarre game of dominoes. The principal was pulling all the beautiful books off a shelf and throwing them across the room while Ash, Nephi, and Parker, who had somehow climbed across the pile, were on the other side and trying to push the bookshelf on the bottom back up.

Esther could see it was also holding the weight of all seven shelves and their books. They would have to be moved somehow before the last one would budge. Ash was straining so hard his whole head was red and blood vessels were popping out in his arms. Nephi was trying to push the shelf up and yelling in frustration.

And then she saw it. A foot and the leg of a brown jumpsuit sticking out from underneath the last bookshelf, and she realized the screaming was Ramona, who was on the other side of the pile of shelves, calling Stanley's name over and over again.

Bubba came to the door, and Sophie yelled at him. "Go down and bring up the medics!" He turned and ran for the stairs.

"What happened?" A calm British voice said. Draven entered the room and took it all in before he climbed over to the other side and tried to help Parker lift the shelves.

Sophie helped the principal throw books. Esther got down on the floor and checked Stanley's leg. It was warm. She tried to pull him, but he didn't budge.

"Careful with the books!" Draven bellowed. Ramona jumped to her feet, scowled at him, crawled to the other side, and began tossing the books.

"A lever, we need a lever!" Esther shouted. Sirens. Esther could hear sirens. One sounded like the police. The other two were different. Then heavy steps up the stairs and Papa J and his friend, Officer Ironpot, burst into the room.

"A lever!" Esther yelled at them over the noise.

Papa J locked eyes with her for a second and ran back down the stairs, yelling. "We need a hydraulic jack, something to lift shelves. Get the fire department upstairs! Medics!"

Ironpot went to the furthest bookshelf, the one that must have been the first domino to go down. He threw books off one side and then he squatted. Esther couldn't believe it. His massive girth must have been hiding muscle. The shelf started to tilt and slide. He growled. Ash joined him, and the shelf moved off to the backside of the pile. They went to the next shelf.

"Ma'am! We need you to leave, ma'am! Everyone, step back." Three firefighters with axes and other tools pushed them out of the room while they filled it.

"Esther, downstairs!" Papa J yelled up the stairs.

"But, Dad!"

"Take Ramona with you and get everyone out of the way! Let us do our job!" He pointed at Ramona, who Esther realized was openly weeping while she looked back into the room.

They gathered out on the porch. Ramona had her arms around her older sister, Desdemona. She pulled a Kleenex out of her black shirtsleeve and wiped her watery brown eyes. Her iron-gray hair had pulled out of her tight bun and stood up wildly, framing her thin face. Ramona's red curls were in place, but black mascara tears ran down her face, and her hands shook as she reached for Draven.

"Ramona, dear, don't get emotional on me. You know Stanley's had a good life," Draven said.

Ramona's mouth fell open, and her eyes narrowed. "He's going to be fine!"

"You have to accept reality..."

Ash stepped between Draven and Ramona, folded his arms, and without saying a word, ended the conversation with a look that Esther was sure could kill. Parker took Esther's hand, but his eyes were on what was happening. Nephi was calm as always, but just like Parker, watching everything unfold.

"Good Gobstoppers, Mr. Kane, what is wrong with you?" Sophie asked. She had a hand on her hip and pointed up at Draven's face. Draven waved her away. Before Esther could stop her, Sophie used both her hands to shove him so hard he took a step back to avoid falling. Esther could swear she saw Ramona's mouth twitch as if she wanted to smile. Desdemona did smile, broadly.

Papa J grabbed Sophie by the back of her shirt before she could have another go at Draven. "Alright, everyone. It's time to work together. Ramona,

I need information about Stanley. I need his name, date of birth, and any medical information dispatch should relay to the hospital."

Esther could hear a power saw running. Draven looked toward the door, his mouth open, and closed his eyes, rubbing his face in what looked like complete frustration.

Draven pointed at the front door. "Officer, those books are valuable."

Papa J spun around and looked so angry that Esther stepped back. "Let's start with you," he said to Draven. Papa J took out a small notepad and pen. Poised to write, he asked, "What is your full name and date of birth, and where were you when the shelves went over?"

"Don't you think it was an accident?" Draven pulled his chin in and leaned toward Papa J.

"Name!"

"Draven Saint Kane."

"You've got to be kidding," Hart said but wrote it down.

"Excuse me?" Draven fisted his hands.

"Date of birth, and where were you?"

"I was in the tiny house behind the store."

Ramona let go of her sister. "What were you doing there?"

"I was fixing the toilet, if you must know. Alvah rents the tiny house behind the store from us. It's our responsibility to do repairs." Draven gave Papa J his date of birth.

Papa J turned to Ramona. "Now, what is Stanley's full name? How old is he, and does he have any medical conditions the hospital needs to know about?"

"He's a diabetic," Ramona said. Papa J talked into the radio piece clipped to his shoulder.

"Stanley Lloyd Brocklehurst, age sixty-seven," Desdemona said. She blew her nose loudly but appeared more composed.

The sounds in the house changed, and Ash went to the door. "They're bringing him down," he said in his deep voice. He motioned for the group to move away from the door.

A gurney bounced down the last of the stairs. Two firefighters were on either end, followed by Officer Ironpot, who carried a piece of equipment and an axe. A medic was holding a tank of oxygen. which was being delivered to a mask over Stanley's face. The other two were holding an IV bag high above Stanley and a large box of supplies and jogging alongside. Ironpot and the firefighters began loading the truck.

Esther was surprised. What she could see of Stanley's face seemed intact. She looked down his body, strapped to the backboard, and realized that there was blood. It was dripping from his right arm. He obviously had a compound fracture.

Ramona and Desdemona ran toward him, but Papa J held his hand up and stopped them while they rolled Stanley off the porch and into a waiting ambulance. Then he let the women follow the gurney. Desdemona climbed in the ambulance, and Ramona ran back up the stairs, into the store, and returned with her purse and car keys.

Within a minute, the ambulance had pulled away, with Ramona and Draven following it. It wasn't until they pulled out that Esther noticed Alvah standing by the door to Literal Buns, watching everything unfold. Alvah locked eyes with her, shook her head, looked down, and walked around the building until she was out of sight.

Two volunteer firefighters hauled another piece of equipment out the door. Ironpot jogged up and helped them by holding the door open before he went back up the stairs.

Papa J turned to Ash. With his pen poised, he said, "You're our new neighbor, aren't you?"

Ash nodded.

"Can I get your name and date of birth?"

"Ash Melvin Corradao, but don't write it down. I'm not going anywhere. I own Literal Buns." He pointed at the sign over the bakery.

"I saw your prison tattoo. Are you on post prison parole?" Papa J asked.

Ash nodded. He seemed to be a man of few words.

"So if I put you in my report, the parole officer has reason to return you to prison to serve out your sentence because you're not allowed to have any contact with law enforcement?"

Ash nodded again.

"Okay. Listen. This is likely just an accident, but it stinks. I know where you work, but if the death is designated a suspicious death, I will have to include you in my report," Papa J said.

Ash's shoulders dropped, and he gave Papa J a single nod of appreciation.

"Can anyone tell me what happened?" Papa J sounded exasperated. "Esther? Anyone?" He looked directly at Esther.

"We heard a crash and ran to see what it was. Well, you saw what we saw," Esther said. "I felt Stanley's leg, and it seemed to be warm or alive, so we started helping Ramona remove the books and tried to move the shelves."

"So Ramona was already up there?" Papa J made a note.

"To be precise, we don't really know. We were in the bakery with Ash, Bubba, Nephi, and Parker when we heard the crash or loud noise of the

63

shelves falling. Ramona could have arrived a second before us, coming from another direction. We all came. Desdemona and Draven arrived shortly after we did. The only two people that didn't come to help weren't scheduled to work. Raini, who left for home earlier, and Alvah, who got off when Raini did. But I did see Alvah standing by Literal Buns, watching it all happen. Then she just walked away. We didn't have an earthquake, and I don't know if you noticed, but those bookshelves were bolted to the floor at some point with metal pieces."

While Papa J was collecting information, Grandma Mable and Marion, their neighbor and a counselor, pulled into the parking lot in Marion's Prius.

Esther took the stairs two at a time and fell, crying, into Grandma Mable's arms.

"I saw it on the social media scanner page," Grandma Mable said. "The uncensored one. I couldn't stay home. I need to call your mom. She wants to be sure you're okay. Mary is asleep or your mom would have come with us."

"Can I join this group hug?" Sophie asked. Grandma Mable gathered Sophie and Marion and held them as tight as they held each other.

"It was awful," Esther said. "Stanley Brocklehurst was in the rare books room when the shelves fell, and he was crushed under the weight. We couldn't get to him until the fire department and Officer Ironpot showed up."

Volunteer firefighters finished loading their equipment, climbed into the fire engine, and pulled out of the parking lot. Ironpot walked toward the group and conferred with Papa J. Esther wanted to get closer so she could hear, but before she could move, Ironpot walked around the house, the same way Alvah had done.

Esther caught Sophie's eye. "Ironpot must be going to check on Draven's story."

"One thing is certain," Sophie said. "This was not an accident. If the bookshelves were bolted, then someone had to remove the bolts before this afternoon. Don't you think?"

"Where is Grandma?" Esther asked.

Sophie pointed. Marion was sitting on the porch swing with Grandma Mable. They were in deep conversation with Ash, who stood over them. Parker, Nephi, and Bubba were back in the bakery.

"Come on," Esther whispered. She walked up the steps, onto the porch, and casually leaned against the wall near the adults. Sophie got a little closer and jumped up to sit on the porch railing.

"I think that's a great idea," Grandma Mable said. "I'll be here early tomorrow. Between you and me, there will always be an adult in the bakery until we get this sorted out."

"Can you work as a barista?" Ash asked.

Marion laughed one guffaw and covered his mouth. "Mable? Coffee? No. Not unless you sell diet coke frappes."

"I worked at The Soup, Smoothie and Tea shop. I may not drink it, but I can make it." Mable snickered.

"I'll train you tomorrow," Ash said. Esther noticed one side of his mouth was pulled up as if it was trying desperately to birth a smile but Ash wouldn't allow it.

Mable nodded. "Also, Ash, I know you had counselors in prison, but Marion here is trauma trained and does EMD... What was that?"

"EMDR," Marion said.

"I know what it is. You should have a session with every single one of these kids," Ash said.

"I'll let their parents know that I'm willing to work with them without charging them," Marion said. A black cat skittered across the porch and jumped onto Marion's lap.

"Look. Marion is a cat whisperer," Sophie said.

"Here comes Officer Ironpot and your dad," Mable said.

Ash looked down at the floor and shuffled his feet. He put his hands in his jeans pocket. The officers crossed the porch.

"Esther, Sophie, you two should get home. The same for Parker, Nephi, and Bubba. It's late," Papa J said. But he was focused on Ironpot and didn't push the issue, and so Esther decided to continue listening in for a little bit longer.

"Well?" Mable asked.

Ironpot nodded. "Alvah says he was with her in the tiny house when the shelves went down."

"He doesn't strike me as someone who would get his hands dirty repairing a toilet," Grandma Mable said.

"He wasn't," Ironpot said and looked at Papa J, and then over his shoulder at the girls. "She said they were doing something different."

"Didn't your dad just tell you to go home? It's practically the middle of the night," Mable said.

Sophie checked her phone. "It's only eight-forty-three."

Ironpot grinned. "Forty-three exactly?"

"Forty-three and thirty seconds now." Sophie put her phone back in her jeans pocket.

Grandma Mable gave Esther the tsk-tsk look and shook her head. "Come on, girls. Let's get the guys and go home."

"But what about Stanley?" Esther asked.

"We aren't going to hear a thing tonight. You can check with Ramona tomorrow."

"Or we can just hack into the hospital," Sophie said.

"I know you would never do that and risk prison time ruining your college prospects," Mable said. Then, as an afterthought, she looked to see if Ash heard her.

He did. He stood up to his full height. "Mable is right. Trust me. Breaking the law is like asking to have all your privileges removed forever over one bad decision."

"I know a little bit about prison. I'm not doing anything that will send me there. I've got the Jeep," Esther said.

"Then get in it." Grandma Mable smiled at her.

"I'll just go get my purse, and then we'll leave. Pinky promise."

"Me too," Sophie said. "I left my school bag upstairs in the office."

"Make it quick," Mable said and went back to her conversation with Ash and Marion.

Esther followed Sophie inside the quiet, ice-cold store. She could hear a furnace blowing air, but the doors had been open, letting all the heat out.

"Shut the door," Sophie whispered.

"Right? I bet her heating bill from tonight is astronomical," Esther said.

"Not that. I want to look at the room."

The girls trotted up the stairs. When they got to the door, the lights were still on. There was a pool of blood where Stanley was trapped. The bookshelf had been destroyed. There were saw marks on the wood. Rare books were scattered in heaps around the room.

Esther walked to the right side of the room, or rather where the first shelf in the bizarre game of shelf dominoes was before the event.

"Look, Sophie. There are metal plates on the bottom shelf with a place for bolts, but no bolts."

"The next bookshelf tore the board right out of the hardwood floor." Sophie pointed and for the first time, Esther realized the extent of the damage to the floor.

"This was intentional," Esther said.

Sophie nodded in agreement. "Biscuits. It can't be Ash Corradao. He was with us."

"Unless he is working with someone else. Someone we don't know," Esther said.

"Like they could still be in the house?" Sophie and Esther stopped moving and listened.

"I don't hear anything. Come on, let's get our book bags, and get out of here."

They ran quietly down the stairs, grabbed their bags from the employee coatrack, and went out on the porch to find Ash talking to Grandma Mable and Marion as an old friend would.

"Thanks for the offer," Ash said. "I will. Let me put my number in your phone."

Marion handed him his phone, and Ash entered his contact info.

"Okay, girls. Marion and I will follow you home. No sneaking off to the hospital," Grandma Mable said.

"What? Sneak? Me?" Sophie put her hands over her heart. Esther roller her eyes.

"Sophie Ito, be careful or your nose will grow," Grandma Mable said.

"She needs something to grow," Nephi said. "Bubba, I'll take you home. Let's get out of here."

8

It was Christmas morning, and Santa, with the clear blue eyes, was driving away. The air was crisp, and the porch was cold under eight-year-old Esther's bare feet.

"Come on! They said we could ride!" Nephi handed her a bike helmet. They strapped them on and adjusted the chinstraps.

"I'm still in my nightgown," Esther said.

"Who cares?" Nephi was still in his superman pajamas with the attached cape. He tried to get the bike down the twelve front steps, but it got away from him and fell onto the lawn. She laughed while he ran to check it for scratches.

"Come help me!" she called.

But he didn't hear her. He was already riding away. She thought about getting her mom, who was examining the presents Santa had delivered, but she had to catch up. She held tight to the handrail and the bike seat, trying so hard. But it landed right where Nephi's had.

She ran the last of the steps onto the wet grass in her bare feet. She checked the bell. The ring was perfect. She rang it again, pushed the bike up, and hopped on.

The gravel road was a little bumpy, but it didn't stop her laughter and squeals of delight. She smiled all the way to her eyebrows. Nephi was stopped up ahead, turned sideways, and was watching her, pumping his fist, whistling, and cheering her on.

There was someone else next to him. Another girl on a bike like hers. Esther hit her brake and slid on the gravel to a stop, jumped off her seat, and held the bike by its handlebars.

"Hi. I'm Sophie, your new neighbor..." She smiled. "I'll race you."

Esther and Nephi hopped onto their bikes, but the tiny girl was already ahead of them, pedaling like a crazy person. Esther pedaled as hard as she could, but the sandy road got softer and softer. It took all her energy to keep pedaling without letting the bike fall over. She tried to call out, but no sound came out of her mouth.

She sat straight up in bed, breathing hard. She smiled, gathered Miss Molly up in her arms, and closed her eyes, drifting away to another dream. *I love Christmas,* she thought.

***

When Esther and Sophie returned to the bookstore, a police cruiser and an unmarked car were parked in front of the store. A handwritten sign on the doors read, "Closed until Wednesday." Ramona greeted them at the front door. She looked as well put-together as usual, but dark circles under her eyes betrayed how tired she was.

Heavy feet walked on the second floor. Esther could hear voices. Chief of police, Lampii, and Officer Neilson walked down the stairs behind an officer Esther didn't recognize.

This was unusual for Esther because her stepfather was an officer. She had met everyone on the small-town police force at one time or another. Necanicum had less than two thousand full-time residents. Vacation homes stood empty in the winter. Esther's school, Oceanside High, had only about five hundred students. So every new face or person stood out like a shark in a fish tank.

The new person was short, muscular, and wore her black hair short on one side and long on the other. Her brown eyes were bright, and she was smiling. While the chief and Officer Neilson were in uniform, she wore street clothes, black dress pants, a black vest, and a black shirt. A plastic ID badge hung on a lanyard around her neck and read Detective Garcia-Smith.

When they reached the entryway, Detective Garcia-Smith turned around, facing the chief and Neilson. "Who processes the crime scene?"

"We do," Chief Lampii said. "We all pitch in and do it ourselves, right, Neilson? You'll get the same annual training we all do."

"I'm trained," Detective Garcia-Smith said. She folded her arms, looked up at the chief, bit her lip, and raised her brows. The look the chief gave the detective reminded Esther of her own Grandmother Mable's famous, don't-underestimate-me-because-I'm-old face.

The chief looked over the detective's head at Ramona. "Ma'am, we've processed the scene as much as we are going to. You're welcome to clean up."

The new detective sighed, and her head dropped. Esther could feel her frustration filling the room.

The detective turned around to face Ramona and forced a smile. "We are so sorry about your experience. An advocate from the district attorney's office will be in touch to assist you through the legal process. Here is my card with your case number written on the back. You are, of course, welcome to reach out to me if you think of anything else. I greatly appreciate all your assistance."

Ramona looked at the card in her hand. "Thank you, detective."

Esther opened the door for the officers.

"Esther James, why am I not surprised to see you here?" Chief Lampii shook his head.

"Hey. It's not our fault," Sophie said.

Officer Neilson winked at Esther, who tried to wink back, but only managed a rapid blink. He had been a good friend to Esther, her family, and friends in the past. Initially, he and her stepfather had hated each other. Later, when lives were at stake, Esther learned that he was the father of the school librarian, Ms. Priest. With a little persuasion from Ms. Priest, he not only came through, but he also cemented a new friendship with her stepfather.

The officers crossed the porch while Ramona and the girls watched.

"Miss Brocklehurst?" Esther asked.

"Yes?" She closed the door, watching the officers talk, then get in their cars, and finally begin driving away.

"How is your brother?" Esther asked.

Ramona bit her lip. "He is in a coma. Desdemona is with him."

"Oh, no," Esther said.

"No, it's good. The doctors put him into a coma because of the seriousness of his head trauma. They say they can bring him back out of it, hopefully."

"How bad are his injuries?" Sophie asked.

"He has some head trauma, but it's hard to tell how bad it is at this point. He has a compound fracture, and his arm was pinned under the shelf for an extended time. Luckily, the room is small, and so the bookshelf hit the wall, and the full weight of it didn't crush him. They also don't know if he suffered any spinal injuries. Right now, they don't see anything on his scans, but we can't be sure until he is awake."

"I hope he heals quickly and is home for Christmas," Esther said.

"Me too. But the trauma will be something that might take some time for him to get over," Ramona said. "Thanks for coming in so early on a Sunday. I wouldn't ask, but we have a buyer for a book, and it's missing. I'm hoping that as we clean up the rare book room, it will show up."

"How are we going to get the shelves up?" Esther asked.

The girls followed Ramona up the stairs to the room that looked just the way it had immediately following the accident, except the blood stain was just a dark smear. Someone had been scrubbing the carpet. A bucket and scrub brush stood by the wet stain.

Ramona picked up the bucket. "Ash said he would help later today. He and I can try to move the shelves back into place. But first we need to organize the books and check for damage."

"Which book is missing?" Sophie asked.

"It's a signed first edition of Agatha Christie's story in *The Strand Magaine*, or a collection of stories. Her story is called, 'The Queen of the Seas.' It is particularly valuable because it was signed by the author and Winston Churchill."

"Wow, that must be valuable," Sophie said.

"We have an offer of thirty-two thousand, but other offers may come in."

She pulled apart clean plastic tubs and handed the girls bubble wrap. "Put a sheet between each book. I will make little signs and we will try to get them gathered by genre and pull out the most valuable of the manuscripts."

Esther picked up a book and read the title. "Jane Austen."

"What is your system for organizing your books?" Sophie asked.

"I have a printed inventory of each section. We don't bring buyers into this room. A lot of what we do is totally online. If we have to show a book, we use the room across the hall." She pointed at a closed door. She picked up a folder and Scotch tape, and began taping the lists to the bins.

"We use our own unique system. For the majority of the books, we separate them by genre and then alphabetize them by the author's name. We don't want to tape anything to our books. I also don't like putting bookmarks or cards inside books. Ink can bleed.

"The books that are highlighted in blue are the rarest and most valuable books we own. They belong on the shelf closest to my office. Once again, by author."

"What about books like this?" Sophie held up a small book.

"When it comes time to shelve books that are large or very small, I'll help and decide the safest way to shelve them."

"Shut the front door!" Sophie put on the white gloves to protect the book she held reverently. Her mouth was opened as wide as her eyes. "It's a first edition copy of *Harry Potter and The Philosopher's Stone*, signed by J.K. Rowling!"

Ramona smiled broadly. "Oh, good. How does it look?" She took the book from Sophie and began examining it closely. "It doesn't look damaged. I am so relieved. One recently sold for over ninety-five thousand."

"Dollars?" Sophie asked.

"Dollars."

Sophie whistled, making Esther chuckle.

"This is like treasure hunting but better. It's for books," Esther said. She picked up another book. "This is a copy of Jane Austen's *Persuasion*. It looks like a first edition, 1918."

"There are three more books in that set. Look for the same spine. *Northanger Abbey* is one of them," Ramona said. "Those also go on the valuable shelf, so bring them to me."

Esther felt like no time had passed at all when her Grandmother Mable let herself in the room.

"I've been knocking on the door, but you didn't hear me," Grandma Mable said.

Ramona looked confused.

"I started working at Literal Buns today. Anyway, Ash said to come over and see if you girls had eaten, and if not, to invite you all to lunch."

"I shouldn't stop. We need to get the store back open," Ramona said.

"The store downstairs just needs a good mop to wipe away any sign of the firefighter's big feet. The girls can help with that. Right, girls?"

"I would rather stay up here and smell all these good books," Esther said.

"I'm starving to death. Bring on lunch." Sophie followed Grandma Mable out of the room, with Esther and Ramona right behind her.

Christmas lights were partially taped to the display case in Literal Buns. Three fake trees of varying sizes stood in the center of the room, waiting to be decorated. Christmas music played, but it wasn't a song Esther recognized.

"No customers?" Ramona asked.

"It'll pick up. Maybe today a little quiet will do us some good," Ash said. "Mable and I are decorating. I taught Bubba how to make shepherd's pie and then sent him home. Would you like a piece with a fresh homemade roll?"

"Can I have two?" Sophie asked.

Ash smiled, and Esther heard him chuckle. He had a deep voice and a deeper laugh. Sophie pulled a chair up to a large table and sat down. Esther sat with her.

Ash looked at Ramona. "Did you lose anything valuable? I know some of those books were worth thousands."

"How did you know?" Sophie asked.

"Has someone shown you the rare books room?" Ramona asked. "If they have, they should have told me."

"I googled, and you have one advertised on the web," Ash said. His face clouded over. He walked back to the kitchen.

"I don't have any books advertised on the web right now," Ramona said to his retreating figure. He didn't turn around to answer her statement. "I've been revamping the website with our new location and information."

"Will your business insurance cover your losses?" Grandma Mable asked.

"Maybe, but that won't help me rebuild my inventory. I've spent years gathering the books I have." She sat at a table with the girls and Grandma Mable.

"Do you want some coffee or water?" Mable asked.

"Both," Ramona said.

"Diet coke, Grandma," Esther said.

"Make it two," Sophie said. "What's playing?"

"*You Sleighed Me, Hipster Holidaze*, on Spotify," Mable did a little jig on her way to make coffee.

"I don't believe in Santa Claus," Sophie said.

Esther smiled. "Good, because he doesn't believe in you either. Coal, Soph, you're getting coal!"

Ramona laughed. "You girls. You keep me young."

The bells on the bakery doors tinkled. Alvah came in and walked to the counter. She was dressed as she had been before, in a Christmas sweater, yet she looked different. Dark circles under her eyes and her sour expression were not hidden by layers of makeup on her face. Her hair looked slept on. Her sweater could have won an ugly Christmas sweater contest. It had red and green bells sewn down each sleeve. One sleeve was green, and the other was red.

"Alvah, join us," Ramona called.

Alvah looked at the tired group. "Can I have a black coffee? Use your biggest mug," Alvah said to Grandma Mable. She walked to their table and slumped into the chair at the end of the table.

"I've been worried about you. You didn't answer my calls," Ramona said.

"Where's Draven?" Alvah asked.

Ramona frowned and looked down. "He drove to Portland for a major book sale."

Alvah didn't reply to Ramona. She took her cup of coffee from Mable and looked at it as though Mable had just handed her a cup of rotten fish.

"When am I scheduled next?" Alvah asked.

"I called because I wanted to know if you wanted an extra shift and to help us clean up the rare books room," Ramona said. She added sugar and cream to her cup of coffee and stirred it while waiting for Alvah's response.

"Yeah. I can help tomorrow. What time do you want me?" Alvah didn't look up. Esther thought Alvah's answer was basically a, no-I-don't-want-to-help-you, answer.

"Your shift starts at ten a.m. and ends when the girls get there after school."

Alvah continued looking into her coffee cup as if she were in a trance.

"Here is Bubba's shepherd's pie." Ash laid a steaming plate in front of Ramona and Mable. The pie was thick and smelled delicious. Cheese was melted across the potatoes on top.

Esther's mouth watered. When her plate of pie appeared, she touched the roll. It was still hot. She took a pat of butter, unwrapped it, and went to work. The roll smelled and tasted better than any bread Esther had eaten in her life. She closed her eyes and savored the first bites.

"Good?" Sophie asked.

Esther opened her eyes to find Sophie laughing at her, along with the entire table. With a mouth full, Esther said, "It's so good."

"I'll take that as a compliment. Alvah, do you want lunch too?" Ash asked.

"No. I have to feed my cat." Alvah picked up her coffee, downed the last of it, and set the mug on the table before she left the bakery.

"That's the last book. Once the shelves are up, we can help you organize them," Esther said.

"Thank you, girls. I was so overwhelmed when I called you. You can't imagine how relieved I am right now," Ramona said.

"But we never found *The Strand* and Agatha Christie's signed story," Sophie said. "Something stinks, and it's not just me."

Esther grinned. "You do stink a little."

"Personally, I'm as concerned about the ink and quills as I am with the book," Ramona said.

Esther pushed one of the book containers closer to the wall. "Are they valuable?"

"I had one silver Egyptian-style inkwell with a Sphynx on it that I thought might be valuable. It's from 1870 and might be worth a few thousand. But truthfully, I wanted to keep it for my bedroom desk. The piece that interested Draven was the teapot-style bottle of ink that looked like it still contained ink. The quills aren't worth much, but I do love them as decorations."

"Where did you find all the cool ink bottles and wells?" Esther asked.

"The Seaside Stories owner sold me some boxes of books, ink, and quills," Ramona said. "I asked if he wanted to appraise them and pay a higher value, but he said to name my price. I felt guilty about the low price I paid. I made my offer, expecting him to ask for more. Maybe that's why I can't find the inkwell and quills anywhere. It's karma."

"Maybe Stanley was storing them before the accident and that's why they aren't here," Esther said.

"Possibly, but I need to get up to the hospital and switch off with my sister. I don't have time to look tonight." She straightened out her back and stretched.

"We can lock the door when we leave," Esther said.

"Thank you. That would be lovely. Then I can go clean up and go to the hospital." Ramona gave the girls a sad smile and left the room.

Esther was dying to know how the rest of the house looked. It felt like a maze of halls and doors. Across from the rare books and manuscript room was a beautiful sitting room that Ramona used when she met with customers. Esther wondered how someone Ramona, who collected fine things, would decorate her bedroom.

"Good. She's gone," Sophie said.

"Soph." Esther shook her head and laughed quietly.

"Seriously. I thought she would never go. I am dying to know what the room across the hall looks like. For all we know, the missing book is sitting on a coffee table."

"Maybe she will show us later. She's..." Esther didn't get to finish her sentence. Sophie was halfway to the other room's door before she caught up with her.

"Sophie," she whispered.

Sophie reached for the doorknob.

"Soph!" Esther tried to pull Sophie's hand off the knob.

"You know you want to look."

She was right. Esther let go and rolled her eyes. "Okay..."

The room was pitch black. Esther felt the wall by the door for a light switch. It had an old knob or button switch that required you to turn it like clock hands, right for on and left for off.

She heard Sophie gasp. "Look at this. It's another signed first edition by J.K. Rowling."

The furniture in the room looked as if it was straight out of the 1800s. Esther half expected Jane Austen's characters to take a turn around the room. A spinet sat on a raised platform. Two camel back couches faced each other. On the table was a bookstand. It was empty but obviously elegant. The wood was carved to look like a peacock spreading his feathers.

Sophie walked over and opened the curtains. "You should see the view. See the lights on Main Street? I bet you can see the ocean from here during the day."

"Sophie!" Esther whispered vehemently. "You're going to get us fired."

"Only if we get caught."

Esther left her in the room and walked back across the hall to pick up the hoodie she had left on the floor in the rare books room. She heard the light button click and turned to see Sophie close the door. She let out a sigh of relief.

"You worry too much, E," Sophie said.

Esther smiled. "Yes, but there is one thing I want to do tonight that might get us fired as well."

"You? Miss Perfection by the Pacific?"

"Hey now. Seriously. I say we go look at the house that they keep talking about. The one behind the bookstore. Draven gives me the shivers. Ramona said he is in Portland buying books, but he doesn't even seem to care about Stanley. All he cared about was the books and money."

"What's the problem with caring about money? I want some," Sophie said.

"Come on." Esther turned the lights off upstairs and walked down the stairs, using the flashlight from her cell phone.

"Don't you hate the short days in December?" It wasn't a question. Sophie was making a Sophie statement of fact.

When they reached the bottom step, the black cat they had seen before ran across the room in front of them.

"Wait. It's bad luck." Esther stopped out of habit.

"Get a grip! I guarantee that cat is not a bad-luck omen." Sophie tripped on the rug but caught herself, straightened her glasses, and zipped up her hoodie.

"Maybe Alvah is still grieving Hazel. Maybe that's why she was so weird after the accident."

"Or maybe she is a mad killer and doesn't care what you think," Sophie said.

They locked up, crossed the porch, and descended to the parking lot, where they headed to the back of the bookstore.

"I don't like Draven. Just because they alibied each other, doesn't mean they are telling the truth," Esther said.

Sophie talked with her hands. "Toilets? Does he strike you as someone who would get on his knees in a bathroom and fix a toilet? I think not." Sophie stopped walking.

Esther followed her eyes and found the tiny house she had heard about yesterday.

Sophie put her hand out and stopped Esther. "Wait. The gravel makes too much noise. Let's go into the trees and look around before we knock on the door."

Before they got close enough to the house to be heard or seen, they moved south and into the pine trees and ferns at the back of the property.

"If we knock on the door, what are we going to say?" Esther asked.

"Leave it to me," Sophie said.

The house had a pitched room and was small enough that it reminded Esther of the witch's cabin in the story of Hansel and Gretel. It had cedar shake or shingled sides and small paned vinyl windows, so it wasn't as old as the main house. The trim was painted white, and unlike the store, it blended into the trees.

Lights were on inside, and the drapes were open, so the girls could see the simple decorations.

Esther heard someone talking. "Shush."

They stood and waited for a moment. "I can't make out the words," Sophie said.

They inched closer.

Alvah walked past the window with a cell phone to her ear. They could see her, but Esther hoped the window would work like a mirror, and she wouldn't be able to see them. Even so, Esther stepped deeper into the shadows of a tree.

"Yes, he's alive... I'm sure... When are you coming back? I'm tired of pretending," Alvah said and wiped her eyes. She looked straight at the girls. Esther took one more step back, and a twig snapped. "Wait. I hear something... I hate this." She walked to the only door Esther could see inside the house and disappeared into what she guessed was a bedroom.

"He wasn't fixing her toilet," Sophie said.

"We don't know that she's talking to Draven."

"I guess so. But I want to find out. We should tell Ramona."

"You think so?" Esther asked. "What would we say? Hey, we think that lady you're trying to help is trying to help herself to your fiancé."

Esther heard someone else walking on the gravel. She motioned to Sophie and put her finger to her lips to quiet Esther. They stood frozen, listening.

Ash Corradao crossed the parking lot. The motion-sensor light on the small house turned on just in time to catch him knocking on her door. He had a plate of something in his hands.

She opened the door and let him in.

After parking in front of the James house, Esther turned the lights off on the Jeep, but neither girl moved. Her hands fell from the steering wheel to her lap. Silent. Thinking.

"What do we really know about your neighbor?" Sophie asked.

"Not enough."

"Crepes."

"We know that he was in prison for something that probably has to do with murder," Esther said. "We know he is still on parole. We know he must be getting money from somewhere because he is spending it. He bought the cottage and the bakery. He stocked and furnished them."

"Or he leased them."

"Either way, he has cash."

"Whose car is that?" Sophie pointed to a car parked across the street next to Ash's cottage.

Esther shrugged. "I don't know. I can't think about anything but poor Stanley."

The door to the James home opened. Warm light spilled out onto the broad front porch. Esther could see her mother's curly hair silhouetted against the light. The porch light was on, but it wasn't bright. It was an ancient light from a ship that looked old enough to have been in World War II. Her mother held the door open and was talking to someone inside.

A tall, well-dressed man nodded at her mother. Esther used the old window crank to roll down her window. Sophie did the same. Hoping her mother didn't see them eavesdropping, she listened, motionless.

"I hope you understand... have to think..." Her mother kept one hand on the doorknob and one foot inside.

The man nodded. "Thank you for your time. We just want to do what's best and what will give her the best opportunity."

"Opportunities don't mean a thing if you're alone in the world or in an unsafe place." Her mother spoke loud enough it carried clearly on the night air.

"Goodnight, Mrs. James." The man descended the stairs and passed the Jeep without looking in their direction. When he started his car, the headlights blinded Esther. The motor sounded as if it belonged on a racetrack as it faded in the distance.

"What was that about?" Sophie asked.

"I have no idea, but if Mom won't tell me, I bet I can get Grandma Mable to."

"I guess I better go back to my house. It's Christmas break soon. Are we going to make fudge?"

Sophie got out of the Jeep and walked in the direction of the Ito house, which was brightly lit and just down the street. Esther sighed and locked the car before going in.

When she opened the front door, Papa J and her mother were in a heated conversation that stopped abruptly.

"Sorry. I didn't mean to interrupt," Esther said. Her mother and stepfather looked at each other and then back at her. Papa J went into the kitchen, and her mother walked toward the stairs.

Grandma Mable was on the couch. Mary and Nephi weren't there. She guessed that her mother had Nephi take Mary upstairs.

"Mom?" Esther asked.

Her mother flinched.

"Mom, what is going on? Who was that?" Esther asked.

"Nothing for you to worry about. You have enough going on." With that, her mother walked to the foot of the stairs, leaving Esther standing with her mouth open.

Esther turned around to face her grandmother. "Do you know what is going on?"

"Don't I always? But that doesn't mean I can share it with you."

Sensing a mystery, Esther frowned in frustration.

Her mother just chucked and went up the stairs.

Papa J made the mistake of coming back into the room to hang up his bulletproof vest.

"Papa J. What was that all about?"

"Your mom threatened me. You're on your own. I had to pinky swear not to tell you," Papa J said.

"Okay, but what about Hazel's death? What else was in the box with the ink and pens?"

"I can't talk to you about the investigation anymore."

"What do you mean?"

"I can't say." Papa J left her in the living room without looking back. Esther followed him up the stairs. He stopped ahead of her. His shoulders slumped.

He turned around and sat on a stairstep, rubbing his hair with his hands until it stood straight up. He looked down at her and closed his eyes. "We have a new detective. I have already been warned that I am in the middle of a major conflict of interest by responding to a crime that you, Mable, Nephi, Parker, and even Sophie could have committed."

Furious, she barked, "What...?"

He held up a hand, interrupting her. "I love you, baby girl. You and I know who the real suspects are. But right now, I have to walk a fine line between being your stepfather and the first officer on the scene of what may still become a homicide."

"You don't think Raini or Ramona did it. And we were with Ash when it happened."

His lips were pressed in a straight line. She didn't know if he was frustrated with her or with the situation.

"Did I get you in trouble again?"

He shook his head rapidly. "No. The person responsible for this is the person who pushed the shelves over, if someone did. I'm tired, and you should get some rest. Christmas break starts the twenty-second, and I know you have some tests to study for. Focus on that. Let us do our job, E. Okay?"

She didn't know what to say.

His right brow rose in question, then he chuckled and started climbing the stairs again.

An ocean breeze blew in the window and across the desk, making Esther put her hand on a stack of papers. When the breeze had passed, she put a painted rock she used as a paperweight onto the papers. She shut her laptop and admitted to herself that she was getting nowhere.

Her phone sat on her nightstand. She flopped onto the bed and picked it up. No texts.

Text to Sophie, Parker, Nephi, and Paisley: *Hi.*

Text from Parker: Smiling face emoji, waving minion GIF

Text from Esther: *Something weird happened. When we got home there was some guy talking to Mom and Papa J. Nephi, did you see him?*

Text from Nephi: *If I did, I wouldn't tell you.* Laughing emoji, laughing emoji

Text from Paisley: *Nephi! Spill.*

Text from Nephi: *I didn't see or hear a thing. JK*

Text from Parker: *We have someone coming for Christmas! Three guesses.*

Text from Sophie: *Santa.* Santa GIF

Text from Nephi: *My elf on a shelf escaped. Maybe he is on his way to wake you up.*

Text from Paisley: *Creepy! I know. Our grandfather is coming to visit from home!*

Text from Esther: *Is that the grandfather that's a Lord something and lives in Britain?*

Text from Parker: *He will insist you call him Papa.*

Text from Sophie: *Lord Papa!*

Twenty texts later, they said, *Night*. Esther wanted to tell them that Papa J said they were all persons of interest in the investigation but didn't want to be a wet blanket. *Oh well. They'll know soon enough.*

Esther wished she was at home, where she could make a murder wall and organize her thoughts. She pulled out her journal. She wrote Ash, Draven, Ramona, Raini, Alvah, Kol. *Wait a minute? Where was Kol? Why hasn't he been by to see what's going on?* She put a question mark by his name and wrote under it, "Where is he?"

Then she wrote two words at the top of two columns: motive and alibi. Ash was first on the list. What would his motive be? Money, and lots of it. But he had an alibi, so she put a check mark in the alibi column. But Sophie could be right. Maybe he was working with someone else.

She darkened Draven's name by drawing over the lines once, twice, and thinking. Then she wrote under *motive*: money, love triangle. If he hadn't been fixing a toilet, what had he been doing? Maybe Stanley had known something and had threatened Draven. But once again, Draven had an alibi. *However,* she thought, *what if Alvah loves him and alibied him when he wasn't really with her?* That made sense to Esther.

Next to Ramona, Esther wrote under *motive* one word: anger. Because of Alvah. Esther couldn't think of anything else to put there. Did Alvah benefit from the death? Did she have as much money as she looked like she had? Maybe she was selling items on the black market? Maybe she was selling stolen books?

Miss Molly jumped onto Esther's bed and laid on her pillow.

"You're right, Miss Molly. It's time for bed. Did you brush your teeth?"

Miss Molly opened one eye, looked at Esther, and went back to sleep.

Esther snuggled deep into her covers and remembered another Christmas when they still didn't have very much.

One of her presents had meowed.

9

———•———

The following day, Esther and Sophie drove back to the bookstore after school. The store was still closed. Esther locked the Jeep driver's side door.

Sophie laughed as she got out of the passenger side door. "I don't know why you do that. The passenger door on this side doesn't lock. It's Necanicum. And besides, if I was a car thief, I would be stealing something better than this rust bucket."

"Hey now. You're going to hurt her feelings." Esther patted the hood before following Sophie to the porch.

Sophie stopped and looked at Esther. "Where are the tall boys, Parker and Nephi? I don't have anyone to insult."

"They aren't that tall. You're just that short. Parker and Nephi made it on the basketball team and have practice."

"Is this the first time Nephi has played basketball?"

"He played youth league basketball. Usually, he is on the wrestling team.

"I can beat him at wrestling," Sophie said.

"Yes, but they don't allow ankle biting." Esther smiled at her.

The warmth from inside the store hit Esther as they entered. She began peeling layers—her coat, the hoodie she wore under her coat, her scarf, and beanie. She left them with her backpack by the coatrack for employees.

"Good, you're here," Alvah said. She was out the door so fast Esther didn't get a chance to say goodbye.

Ramona came down the stairs with Raini. "Thanks for helping me, Raini. We should be done with everything by tomorrow and resume our regular schedule."

"Great. Thanks for giving me the extra shift," Raini said.

"Hi." Esther smiled at Raini, who smiled back and went to the kitchen and into the fridge.

"Hey. Have you seen Kol?" Esther asked.

"Yes. He's around," Raini said.

"I haven't seen him."

"He's busy."

Esther followed Raini out onto the porch, hoping to get more than short responses to her questions.

Two squad cars and an unmarked police vehicle pulled into the parking lot.

Ramona joined her on the porch. "Oh good. I called this morning and reported some missing items as stolen."

"Do you really think they were stolen?" Esther asked.

"I'm not sure, but I need to let the buyer know there is a delay, and I was told to report it to my insurance company."

The officers got out of their vehicles but didn't say hello. They stood by their squad cars, waiting. Esther recognized the baby-faced officer but couldn't remember his name. Papa J wasn't with the officers. The other two were older men—Davenport and Jones. The baby-faced officer's badge said his name was Finch. Besides looking as if he should be in junior high school, he wasn't more than an inch taller than Esther, or about five-foot eight-inches tall.

Fascinated, they watched as Detective Garcia-Smith got out of the unmarked vehicle and made eye contact only once before she pulled out some papers and walked to the porch.

"Ramona Brocklehurst, I have a search warrant for your building, your vehicle, and employee vehicles. The search warrant also includes your small rental house behind the store and the Literal Buns bakery."

Ramona's brows drew together, and she frowned at the officer. "I'm the one who reported my book and items missing."

"The search is regarding the attempted murder of Stanley Brocklehurst," the detective said.

Ramona deflated. She pulled the door open and waved them in. "Come on in."

Parker, Nephi, and Bubba pulled into the parking lot. Bubba jumped out of the car and began walking away.

Parker and Nephi joined the girls on the porch. Parker gave her a quick hug and then, eyes narrowed, looked through the open door into the store. He shook his head.

"Are you alright?" Parker asked.

"I'm okay." Esther tried to smile and reassure him. He took her hand. Something about Parker, Esther didn't know what, spread peace and a warmth through her whenever he was near. With one simple touch, everything in her world was warm and light, even when the whole world seemed to be coming apart.

"I'm fine too," Sophie said.

"Except you're short," Nephi said. His goofy grin made Esther smile.

"And proud of it, Sasquatch." Sophie gave him a friendly push.

"We need to go to work, but if anything happens, we're here. Promise," Parker said.

"Good," Sophie said. "Then we can provide you with emotional support." She wiggled her eyebrows.

Chuckling, Parker gave Esther one more hug. Nephi shoved Sophie back, almost knocking her over.

"Hey!" she exclaimed.

"Sorry. Here. Let me help you." Nephi picked her up like a baby and rocked her.

"Child abuse! Put me down." Sophie was laughing, and the air was suddenly lighter. Nephi set her on her feet and jogged to catch up with Parker to work in the bakery.

Ash was at the door to the bakery, watching the friends with a sideways smile. The police didn't allow the girls to go inside the store.

Esther leaned close to Sophie and whispered. "Look, he's smiling."

"He should do it more often. He would look a lot less like a serial killer."

"What about Kol? He isn't here," Esther said.

Sophie shrugged. "I'm not going to rat him out. Besides, he wasn't here when Stanley got hurt."

"I haven't seen him for days."

"He is only on the schedule when we aren't. He doesn't have very many days this month."

"I wonder why," Esther said.

Sophie laughed softly. "Really? He's such a pleasant person."

"You're being sarcastic, right?"

"Definitely."

Two hours later, the detective and the officers emerged from the house. Esther didn't see any evidence bags. The officers huddled, and Davenport and Jones went inside Literal Buns.

Ash stood at the door with his arms folded, and for the first time, his expression was easy to read, angry and anxious all at the same time. He flexed the muscles in his jaw, frowning, brows drawn together. He began pacing back and forth just outside the door to Literal Buns.

Esther and Sophie sat on the porch swing, going back and forth slowly. Nephi and Parker waited on a bench outside the bakery. Ramona waited outside the door to the store, alert, like the black cat that sat at her feet. Esther looked at Parker, still amazed that someone so handsome would love her. As if he read her mind, he looked up and smiled. She smiled but quickly looked down at her feet.

The sound of breaking glass came from the bakery.

"Be careful," Ash said through clenched teeth.

"He's angry," Esther said.

"Wouldn't you be?" Sophie asked.

"Hey," Ash barked. "Get out of my kitchen!" He strode into the bakery.

"They could destroy his flour and supplies if they put their hands into it. I wonder how they search a kitchen," Esther said.

"Crepes. I wonder when I will ever get my hands on another mouth-watering cinnamon roll. We need Literal Buns open."

The detective looked over her shoulder at the girls. She pointed, and the younger officer crossed the porch and held out his hand to Esther. "I need a key to your vehicle."

"What are you looking for?" Esther pulled the key out of her jeans pocket and handed it to him.

He didn't answer. He crossed the parking lot and opened the Jeep. First, he searched through her glove box, and then thankfully, it looked as if he had neatly stacked everything back inside. He glanced up at her, and she realized his face was red with embarrassment. He moved the front seats, looked under the dash, popped the hood, and examined the engine compartment.

"Whatever they're looking for, it's small enough to fit in a glove box or be hidden in an engine compartment," Esther said.

"The bolts," Sophie said.

Esther nodded in agreement.

The officer moved to the backseats of the vehicle. He pulled the seat cushions up, as he would if he were going to fold the seatbacks down and make more cargo room.

"Detective! Come look at this," Finch said.

"Biscuits!" Sophie said. She shook her head and looked at Esther. "What did he find?"

Eyes wide, Esther shrugged. "I don't know."

"I hope it's Nephi's three-year-old gym socks."

Finch began taking pictures with a cell phone of whatever he found in the stowaway compartment under the seats. When no one emerged from the house or the bakery, the officer looked back at her and then went to the door of the store.

"Detective!" he yelled. Then he turned and watched them.

"What is it, Finch?" the detective walked out the door. The officer leaned in and spoke to her with his back to the girls. The detective walked briskly to the Jeep with the officer on her heels. Ramona stayed at the door but looked at Esther with her head tilted and her eyes drawn together in confusion.

Esther shrugged and held her breath.

The detective took more pictures. They made notes.

"I can't hear what they're saying." Esther said. Ash came out of the bakery door, followed by Nephi and Parker. Parker jogged up the stairs and took her hand as they waited.

Finch went to the patrol vehicle and opened the trunk. The detective stared at Esther.

"Why is she giving us the stink eye?" Sophie scowled.

"Not us. Me," Esther said and realized she was shaking. Nephi stood closely behind her. Sophie took her other hand.

The officer rushed back with what looked like an orange fish and tackle box. He opened it and pulled out a brush.

"Fingerprints," Parker said.

Ash exhaled so loudly she heard it on the porch. Esther glanced at Ramona, but her back was to Esther and her arms were folded.

Finch went back to the trunk and came back with an evidence bag. The detective put a second set of gloves on. Finch held the bag open.

The detective picked up a book in a Ziploc bag from the stowaway compartment and held it up so Ramona could see it before putting it in the evidence bag.

"Shut the front door!" Sophie said loud enough that Ash's head snapped around. Ramona walked toward the Jeep, but the detective passed her and marched over to Esther. She stopped several feet away, examining Esther's friends.

"Excuse me." Detective Garcia-Smith motioned for Esther's friends to step back. Finch joined her on the porch and invited Sophie and the others to get off the porch and wait with him. Esther stood, shaking and waiting.

Something was happening deep in the pit of Esther's stomach. Fear was triggering adrenaline, and as it usually did with Esther, fierce anger—anger usually foreign to her and almost impossible to control.

"Aren't you Joe Hart's kid?" the detective asked.

Esther's eyes narrowed, but she didn't respond. She had read enough Agatha Christie and been in trouble often enough, due to her curious nature, that she knew better.

"What's your name?"

Esther folded her arms.

"Esther James," Ramona said, walking across the porch to stand by the officer. "Esther? Did you do this?"

Appalled that she even needed to ask, Esther held her mouth in a firm line when she wanted to lash out.

"You need to go with officer Finch, Miss James," the detective said.

"Then you should take me too. We ride together. If she goes to jail, we go together," Sophie said.

"Well, now. You have a point. Finch!" The detective barked, causing Finch to jump. He pulled handcuffs out and put a hand on Esther's shoulder, trying to turn her around. She yanked her shoulder back.

Parker, fists clenched, took a step toward her. Nephi was right behind him. She mouthed no and shook her head once. Parker froze. Nephi ran into Parker's back. The muscles on Nephi's chiseled face were clenching his jaw, fists ready for a fight.

"You don't need to use handcuffs," Parker barked.

"Good grief, Finch. Are you that much of a rookie? Here." The detective took Esther's arm, spun her around, and cuffed her quickly.

"Officer! No need to be hostile!" Parker said.

"Don't forget me." Sophie held her hands out. Finch turned her and cuffed her.

"You're making a serious mistake. You're arresting the girls who are better detectives than you," Nephi growled.

"Do you really need to do that?" Ramona asked. "Esther's a sweet girl. I just don't think she would steal from me."

Finch spoke to dispatch over his radio as he walked them to the squad car and, protecting their heads, put them in the back seat. He got in and rolled his window down.

The detective leaned over. "You don't need your lights, Finch. I know you like them, but not this time."

Draven Kane pulled up alongside the patrol car and leaned out of the open driver's side window of his Mini Cooper. "Officers, what is going on?" Draven asked.

"We found your missing book, Mr. Kane. Thanks for reporting it missing. Oh, yes, and we found the missing bolts," the detective said.

"Gobstoppers," Sophie whispered. "I thought he was in Portland. That's garbage."

Esther turned and looked at Sophie, eyes wide, feeling as if she was going to have a heart attack and throw up all at the same time.

"It's alright, E. We've been here before," Sophie said.

Esther closed her eyes and groaned. "Is that supposed to make me feel better?"

"It's always better to be prepared for what is ahead of you in life. Our expertise will come in handy. I promise." Sophie gave Esther a cheesy grin. That was it. All the anger became ridiculously inappropriate giggles.

As Finch drove away, Esther turned in her seat and watched Draven Kane get smaller. "Sophie, look."

Esther could still see a devilishly broad smile on his face and a dark twinkle in his eye.

10

— • —

Finch brought them into the station from the back of the building and checked them into two interview rooms that had a thin wall between them. He removed the handcuffs but locked the rooms.

Esther sat on the metal bench and leaned against the wall. "Sophie, can you hear me?"

"This wall is so thin. I could probably push hard and see you too."

"Papa J is going to kill me."

"He'll kill someone when he hears you're at the police station, but it won't be you," Sophie said.

The sound of a buzzer interrupted their conversation. Chief Lampii's face appeared in Esther's window. She got up to look out the small window and saw him check on Sophie. A minute later, Papa J was buzzed in and joined the chief on the other side of the door. Esther put her ear against the cold steel door to listen.

"Now, don't get upset, Hart," Chief Lampii said.

"I am already upset," Papa J said. "She didn't have to cuff the girls to bring them in. They aren't a flight risk or violent. I am sure we can get this straightened out."

"There's no need. Ramona Brocklehurst will not cooperate with the theft charges. She wants the girls released."

Shocked, Esther stood and looked out the window in the door. Papa J looked in her direction.

"What about the book?" Papa J asked.

"The book and the bolts were in a bag with fingerprints on it, but none of them belonged to the girls. We already had their fingerprints on record from when all that stuff went down with Ashley," the chief said.

Esther flashed back to how frightened she had been when her friend had been killed. She and Sophie had wrongfully been taken to jail as suspects. Now here she was again.

Mom is going to kill me, Esther thought. "How do we get into these messes, Sophie?"

"Because the world is lucky to have two girls with brains like ours, because Detective Garcia-Smith is going to make a mess of this without us." Sophie spoke so loudly the chief could hear her in the hallway.

"Sophie!" Papa J exclaimed.

"What? The truth hurts, doesn't it?" Sophie said.

"Your mother is in the lobby," Chief Lampii said.

Silence.

The chief chuckled. "Look, Hart. Take the girls home. We're going to record everything and keep it because of Stanley's injuries, but Garcia-Smith said the girls are alibied for the accident. I don't suppose I have to say now is not the time to take that trip to Mexico you've been wanting to go on?"

"Australia. Surfing in Australia," Papa J said while shaking his head at Sophie's cell door.

"There's a lot of sharks in Australia, aren't there?"

"Safer than it is here."

The chief patted Papa J's shoulder and said, "Take the girls home."

Sophie's mother and father waited in the glassed-in lobby of the small Necanicum Police Department. Her mother was frowning when the girls walked into the lobby. One look at Sophie and her frown melted into a mother's look of concern and a hug.

"Mom, I'm fine," Sophie said.

"You're still my little girl, and you could have gotten hurt. You were arrested for murder," her mother said.

"Your mother's right," Mr. Ito said. "You need to come home. We need to talk."

"Talk?" Sophie's mouth fell open, and her glasses slid down her nose. She yanked them off.

Esther waved weakly. "Bye, Sophie. Papa J? I need to go back to Sandy Stories and get the Jeep."

"I believe you also owe Miss Brocklehurst, your boss, a serious thank you."

Papa J drove Esther back to the bookstore in his patrol car. They rode silently for the first minute or two. Then Esther broke the uncomfortable silence.

"I really am sorry," Esther said.

"Why? None of this is your fault," Papa J said. "No one that knows you is stupid enough to believe you took that book. Miss Brocklehurst barely knows you, and she stood up for you. You should thank her, not me."

"I need to talk to Sophie, but I think I know how the book got into the Jeep."

"You know that when you get curious and start solving mysteries, you worry us. It puts you in serious danger."

"I know but..." Esther trailed off.

Papa J parked the police car next to Esther's Jeep. "Let's go thank Miss Brocklehurst before you leave."

"She's supposed to open the store tomorrow. If I still have a job, I should be here helping. Sophie should too."

"Let's see what she has to say."

"This feels like the time Nephi ate candy at the candy store and then didn't pay for it and we both got into trouble," Esther said.

Papa J smiled and then knocked on the shop door. The black cat rubbed on Esther's leg, so she picked her up and petted her. She heard footsteps on the stairs and then saw Ramona through the window coming to the door. Her face was sad, but she smiled. She opened the door and let them in.

Esther wondered if Ramona's next words would be that they were fired and thanks for stopping by. After setting the cat down, she followed Ramona to the fireplace with Papa J.

"Esther. I'm glad you came back," Ramona said.

"Thank you so much for trusting Sophie and me. I promise, we wouldn't steal anything ever," Esther said.

Esther heard footsteps on the wooden staircase. She looked up just in time to see Kol come down the stairs, petulant like rolling thunder. He looked at Esther through narrowed eyes that were so angry she waited for him to growl at her, but he left the store instead.

She turned back to Ramona. "Anyway, I understand if you don't want us to work for you anymore."

"Esther, the last few days have been some of the most difficult of my life." Ramona tucked an errant red curl behind her ear, smiling sadly. "Not once have you done anything in this store except a wonderful job. You've been kind, thoughtful, and, more importantly, jumped in when there was a crisis. Nothing about you makes me think you are capable of that level of deception. I'm a fabulous judge of character, usually, and my thought is that someone is trying to take the heat off themselves by setting you up."

Surprised, Esther took a step back and then thought carefully about her response. "Ramona, I appreciate your level of trust in Sophie and me. We won't disappoint you, I promise. I have no idea how the book got into my car, and since it doesn't lock, someone could have hidden it in there a week ago and I wouldn't have known."

"Exactly. So! I still have a lot to do before we open tomorrow. Christmas break is coming quickly, and we want to make as many sales as possible."

Esther nodded. "We get out at noon the Thursday before Christmas."

"Kol has agreed to work your shift tomorrow, and Raini will stay late to give you a rest. Would you be willing to return to work with me and take his shift?

Relief flooded Esther. It wasn't that she needed to work. It was because she had learned to love the bookstore, and if she was honest with herself, every part of her wanted, no needed, to solve this mystery.

"I'll call Sophie, and if everyone agrees, I will see you Thursday after school," Ramona said.

"Thank you. Can I ask...?"

Papa J's hand on Esther's shoulder stopped her. "We appreciate your call to the chief and not pursuing the stolen book and keeping Esther out of juvenile detention. But I imagine you could probably use a rest after today. I am glad all your stolen items came back, but I'm concerned for your safety, Miss Brocklehurst."

"I will be fine. I'm a big girl," Ramona said. "We need to get the store opened back up."

"Thank you again," Esther said.

"See you tomorrow after school," Ramona said and gently shut the door.

Esther felt the last bit of tension leave her body.

"Now to go home and talk to your mother," Papa J said.

Just like that, all the tension returned.

"Don't worry," Papa J said. "I don't think she's capable of murder either."

11

E sther's mother was on the phone when they came into the house. She looked up when she saw Papa J and Esther, and took her call into the kitchen.

Grandma Mable entered from the kitchen. "How are you?"

"I'm fine," Esther said.

"Tough as nails. That's what you are. Do you have any idea who put the book in your car?" Grandma Mable asked.

The front door opened, and Sophie came in.

"I thought you would be grounded for life," Esther said.

"So did I," Sophie said. "Instead, I have dish duty, and they actually said they understood it wasn't our fault."

"Then why do you have dish duty if they realize we didn't do anything wrong?"

Sophie shrugged.

"Mom?" Her mother reemerged and made a face at Grandma Mable, indicating that Esther's mom needed a moment to talk to the girls alone.

"Call me if they scare you," Grandma Mable said to Esther and Sophie. Chuckling, Grandma Mable went back into the kitchen.

"Sit down," her mother said to the girls.

Neither of them sat.

Esther began twirling one of her curls and chewing on her lip, waiting to be grounded for life or forced to quit sleuthing.

"Mom, I can explain," Esther said.

"Sit down, Esther. We have something more important to talk about. I mean, what just happened is important, but this is different."

As she sank into her seat and Sophie sat next to her, Esther asked, "Mom, is everything okay?"

Her mother seemed distant and frazzled. Papa J sat next to her mother.

"Do you remember anything about before?" Her eyes bore a hole into Esther's soul.

"Before?"

"You know. Before the divorce, before your dad went to prison."

"I was really little. I have a few memories. I remember going water skiing or tubing in a lake and staying in a cabin. I remember a few Christmas mornings, but no real details. I remember learning to ride my tricycle, actually. That's my oldest memory. Why?" Esther searched her mother's face.

"Do you remember whose cabin we stayed in?" her mother asked.

"No. It was a really nice cabin."

Her mother smiled. "It really was, wasn't it? Do you remember any people there besides your dad?"

"No."

Her mother took a deep breath and blew it out slowly.

"Mom, just say it."

"Your grandfather passed away." Her mother sat back and watched Esther's face.

Sophie stood close to Esther and gave Esther's hand a quick squeeze, letting Esther know she was there, and then gently put the same hand on Esther's back.

Esther's brows drew together in confusion. She leaned forward and tipped her head. "My grandfather? Grandma Mable's husband has been dead for a long time."

"Not Grandpa James. Grandpa Day, your father's father." Her mother looked back and forth from Esther's eyes to Papa J's.

"So? I never knew him. Are you worried that I'll be sad?"

"Not exactly," her mother said. "Your uncle is in town."

"Wait. I have an uncle?" Esther asked.

"Please, Esther, for right now, if anyone approaches you and says they're family, ask them to wait to talk to you until I can be present. Okay?"

"Did he try to kill Stanley?" Sophie asked.

"Mom. I'm old enough to—" Esther said.

"Esther." Papa J interrupted her. He shook his head, ever so slightly, and then looked at her mom. Esther knew what he was saying. He wanted her to respect her mother.

"Okay. Is he dangerous? What's his name? Was he the man at the house the other night?"

"Wait! It isn't Ash, is it?" Sophie asked.

Her mother fell back in her chair. "No. He hasn't been to the house, he is not Ash, and he's not dangerous. His name is Mustang Dee Day. Thank you, Esther. You won't regret it, I promise."

I am already regretting it, Esther thought. But at least I have a name to google.

Mrs. Hoffman left the store with her shopping basket full of books. Esther watched her juggle her cane and the books expertly, but she had still passed her and held the door open for her.

"I can open my own door, Esther."

"Sorry, Mrs. Hoffman."

"I'm not dead yet, you know."

"Yes, Mrs. Hoffman. Merry Christmas."

"I'm Jewish, Esther." Mrs. Hoffman shook her head back and forth as she passed Esther and crossed the wooden front porch.

"Happy Hanukkah, Mrs. Hoffman!" Esther waved.

Mrs. Hoffman rolled her eyes and loaded her literary treasures into the back of a Volvo. "Happy Hanukkah to you!"

Surprised, Esther beamed. She closed the door and turned the sign to closed.

"Are you ready?" Sophie asked.

"Of course. But we haven't seen Ramona all day. I feel like we should check in with her before we take off." Esther turned the overhead lights off, leaving the string of Christmas lights and holly on the mantle and the Christmas trees lit.

The girls retrieved their matching coats from the coatrack and put on their backpacks.

Esther looked up the stairs. The lights were on in the rare book room. Neither one of them had ventured up during their shift. It had been a busy evening in the store.

"I think I sold more books tonight than any other," Sophie said.

"I was worried, with everything that happened to Stanley, the store would lose customers. Let's go see if she is in her office. Come on."

"As long as we don't miss the donuts and cider."

Holding the railing, Esther quietly climbed the stairs and peeked into the rare books room. The lights were on, and Ramona was kneeling on the floor by the shelf closest to her office, the shelf that held the most valuable books. Paper and a pen were on the floor next to her. She was closely examining the binding of a small leather book.

Esther waited to see if Ramona would look up and see her. Ramona made a note on the paper and then jumped, putting her hand over her heart.

"Oh! Esther. You scared me." Ramona got on her knees and gradually rose and stretched. "What time is it?"

"It's six," Esther said.

"Oh my. I totally lost track of time." She took out her phone, looked at it, and then back up at the girls and smiled. "I will walk you out."

"Are you coming to the Parade of Lights?" Esther asked.

Ramona tilted her head and looked at Esther, questioning. "I heard a little bit about it from one of the nurses, but I am still not sure what it is."

"It's amazing. Next year the store and bakery should have a float, or at least a big truck with Christmas decorations. Would you like to come with us?" Esther asked.

Ramona smiled, but her eyes had circles under them, and Esther was sure she had lost some weight. "I wish I could. I need to go up to the hospital and give Desdemona a break and pick up some Thai food for the both of us. Take pictures and tell me all about it tomorrow."

"Okay. But they serve the best cider and donuts at the end of the parade. You're missing out," Sophie said.

"I think Ash makes the best of everything, so I should be just fine. I am going to go get changed into some fresh clothes."

The girls watched Ramona walk to her private quarters in the back of the house.

"Okay, let's get the guys and get out of here." Sophie put her beanie on, adjusted her backpack, and took the stairs at a run.

"I love the parade," Esther said as she worked to keep up. "Do you have your key out?"

Sophie nodded and, after Esther was on the porch, locked the door and checked it twice to make sure it was locked. Then together, they crossed the porch, took the stairs, and knocked on the doors to Literal Buns.

The lights inside went out one by one. Then the Christmas lights outside went off, leaving the girls in the dark. Ash was the first one out the door with a plate covered in tinfoil and a bow. He held the door open for Nephi and Parker. Nephi carried Ash's dog, Cookie, and Parker locked the door.

"Do you want to ride with us?" Parker asked Ash.

"I'll take my own wheels in case I want to leave early. Can you put Cookie in her doggie car seat?"

Sophie snorted and then covered her mouth.

"Is something funny?" Ash asked.

Sophie shook her head but kept her hand tight over her mouth.

"No one makes fun of Cookie," Ash said.

Esther stepped back. The boys carried Cookie to Ash's car, a vintage Ford Bronco with a soft-top. A dog carrier was buckled in the passenger seat. It was more of a padded cube with a window on the front than anything solid. Cookie climbed across the car and into the carrier. She knew it well.

"See you at the house." Ash started the car and drove away, leaving the group standing in the parking lot.

"Nephi? What did he mean by *see us at the house*?" Esther asked.

"We invited him to go to the Parade of Lights with the family, and he said yes," Nephi said.

"Shut the front door!" Sophie exclaimed. "What if he is the killer?"

"All I know is he makes killer cinnamon buns."

"And that erases all crime?" Esther asked.

"They are really good." Sophie licked her lips. "Let's get out of here."

12

— • —

E sther's family and her friends were gathered in her living room, all wrapped up in coats, hats, gloves, scarves, and anything warm.

"Grandma Mable? Are you an elf?" Sophie asked.

Grandma Mable had on green and white striped tights, a red velvet skirt, a plush velvet coat, and a red and white striped hat with pointy ears sewn on the side.

"No. Why?" Grandma Mable cackled. "I'm Santa's helper."

"She's an elf," Mary said. "Me too."

"You're an imp," Sophie said.

"Mom! Sophie called me an imp," Mary wailed.

"It's a term of endearment, Mary, darling," her mother said. The boys chuckled, and the girls made faces at each other.

"What are we waiting for? Are your parents coming, Sophie?" Papa J asked.

"My mother hates being cold. If they come, they will drive and bring our dog, Spam, with them."

"Someone new is going with us," Grandma Mable said.

As if on cue, someone knocked on the door. Grandma Mable plowed through the crowd and opened it. Ash Corradao stood on the porch, with a plate of the most beautiful Christmas cookies Esther had ever seen. He was dressed in all black but had a red and white striped scarf around his neck. Cookie had a matching scarf and a black leash.

"Ash! Those are gorgeous." Esther's mother took the plate of cookies back to the kitchen.

"Thanks, man." Papa J offered Ash his hand, and they shook.

"Well, let's get this show on the road." Grandma Mable opened the door and waved for everyone to leave.

"I can take some in my car," Ash said.

Grandma Mable's infectious laugh was louder than usual. "We walk! It's tradition."

Esther's smile slowly spread until her dimples popped. She reached for Parker's hand.

"Your head is going to get cold," Sophie said to Ash.

"I will run in and get a warmer jacket for me and Cookie."

It was a bright night. The old-fashioned streetlamps outshone the stars and provided a clear path across the sidewalk to Ash's cottage. The group laughed and gathered on the sidewalk while he went in for a coat.

Several things about Ash made Esther wary, including his prison sentence. She watched him walk the stone path to the front door, switch on a light, and go deeper into the small house. There were no curtains, so with the lights on, Esther could see the living room. Her curiosity drove her to get closer. She took a step toward the house, and then another.

The living room was clean and yet homey. He had a large leather sofa and chair by a river rock fireplace. She wasn't surprised to see the chandelier over the coffee table was made of sheds from antlers.

"Nice house," Sophie said.

Esther jumped and put her hand over her heart. "Sophie, you scared me."

"What are you looking for?"

"I don't know, but I'll know it when I see it."

A door opened, and Ash crossed the living room to the front door, right past a desk.

"Sophie," Esther hissed. "Look. He left it sitting in plain sight. Shush. Here he comes." A large, sterling silver inkwell, the shape of a sphinx, shone brightly on a dark wood desk.

"Biscuits. Act casual," Sophie said.

Ash locked his house, smiled, and nodded when he passed the girls.

The Promenade ran the length of the beach, from Esther's street to Parker's family's mansion in the cove. It also served as a sea wall, making everyone in town feel safe because the wall could hold back the ocean. The truth was, Esther had seen the waves wash over the Prom wall and, in a strange way, loved storms. They would have to walk a mile to get to Main Street.

They were not the only group walking in the cool night air. Lamp posts that were as old as Esther's Victorian home were wrapped in Christmas lights and decorated with a single wreath and ribbon. They lit the Prom, making it feel safe.

"You would think on a cold December evening the town would be empty," Parker said.

"I keep forgetting this is your first Christmas in Necanicum," Esther said. "Summer people who own vacation homes return for the holidays."

"I kind of like it when the roads are empty and so are half the houses. It's quiet, and we have the entire beach to ourselves." He squeezed her hand and smiled down at her.

Sophie began making kissing sounds behind them.

Parker laughed. "Sophie, you're the best chaperone ever." Esther looked over her shoulder and grinned at her.

Neighbors passed them, saying hello and catching up on local gossip. To Esther, it felt like a river of joy, people flowing in the same direction, weaving in and out while laughing and talking.

The group passed Malva Peabody, who lived at the end of Esther's street. She was notorious for swearing at neighbors she thought drove too fast through her cul-de-sac. Malva zeroed in on the new face and his dog.

"What have we here?" Malva asked.

Grandma Mable stepped between Malva and Ash. "Malva, this is our new neighbor, Ash Corradao, and his dog, Cookie." Grandma Mable patted Ash on his muscular shoulder.

"I see." Malva didn't offer anything else. Nose in the air, she walked steadily and slower than Esther's group, falling behind.

"Wait for me!" Marion called.

Esther stopped and looked to see Marion trotting up the street. When he got close enough, he took Mable's arm and began whispering in her ear. They laughed like besties, sharing a secret.

Parker started talking football with Nephi. Esther's little sister had Sophie's full attention as she clung to Sophie's hand, listing everything she wanted for Christmas. The group spread out as they walked, leaving Esther walking near Ash in silence with Parker beside her. *Now, maybe I can get an answer to some of my questions.*

Ash didn't look at her. He laughed at Sophie's attempts to get away from Mary's cheerful chatter. Sophie jumped onto Nephi's back, and he gave her a piggyback ride. Mary ran behind him, begging for a ride too.

"The Christmas lights have been lit downtown since the day after Thanksgiving. Why have the parade?" Ash asked.

"Tradition. You know? The town is almost one hundred and fifty years old. There are pictures of tonight's event in the museum dating back to the early 1900s. It's the official tree lighting ceremony. You'll see. It's fun," Esther said, looking down, walking near Ash while taking Parker's hand.

"This is my first Parade of Lights too, man. Same for Paisley, my twin." Parker pointed at his sister, who was walking alongside Nephi. "We moved in last year, after the holidays."

They walked in silence, accompanied by the roar of the ocean as waves rolled in and back out, over and over again. Seagulls sat silently on the lampposts, perched for the night, and a light mist blanketed the world and made Esther's hair curl more than ever.

"So, Ash, what brought you to Necanicum?" Esther asked.

"I came into some money and wanted to start my own bakery. I saw this place online, and the rest is history."

"What bakery did you work in before coming here?" Esther asked.

"Wow. There's a lot of people out," Parker said, interrupting the conversation.

"Should we have chairs?" Ash asked.

Esther smiled insincerely at Ash. "No. We just need to get down near the town square and the tree. There is a little shop that sells the best hot chocolate ever. We always get a hot cup to keep our hands warm during the parade.

Close to Main Street, Esther heard a skateboard coming up behind them. She turned just in time to see Kol fly by, weaving dangerously between people and turning onto Main. Before the turn, he looked over his shoulder, scowling in her direction, black hair flying in the wind.

"Nice," Esther said. Parker shook his head.

The group wove its way through the crowd, stopping occasionally to chat. Esther and Sophie gave their favorite librarian, Ms. Priest, a hug and said hello to her father, Officer Neilson. When they made it to the square, Madison Merriweather; her daughter, Bridget; Parker's parents; and the Stuarts, who had chairs, were waiting near a tree. Esther realized this would also be the first parade for the Stuarts and Madison.

She checked her pocket for the money she had put into it before leaving the house. "Let's go get a hot chocolate," she shouted over the noise to Sophie and her friends.

They made their way across the street from the town square into the Cuppa Coffee Shop. It was small; the crowd and heat steamed the cheerful front windows. The line wound out the door and down the block.

"This must be good," Parker said.

Esther smiled up at him. "You're going to love it."

"Oh, am I?" He laughed.

"If you don't, I'll drink it," Sophie said.

The shop's double glass doors were open, letting in the night air, but it was still hot and muggy with all the bodies pressed close together.

"Hi, Jenna!" Esther waved at the barista and shop owner.

"Hot chocolates? Let me count," Jenna said.

One by one, Jenna handed them steaming cups of cocoa with a swirl of whip cream, a candy cane stir stick, and shaved pieces of chocolate on top. Esther's was so hot she put it in a sleeve.

"Wow. That's beautiful," Parker said.

"Wait until you taste it." Esther stirred her cocoa with her candy cane, watching it melt into the hot liquid. When the crisp fifty-degree night air met the warm cocoa, it steamed and warmed her hands.

They found their way back to their parents. Nephi brought Mary a cup of cocoa. She was wrapped in a Christmas blanket, sitting in one of the Stuarts' chairs on her mom's lap. Esther's mom and Parker's mom were deep in conversation.

A fire engine's siren gave a quick burst of sound a few blocks away, and the crowd cheered, lining up on the sidewalks and curbs. The parade was led by the oldest fire engine in town, and looked as if it should be in an old movie. Flashing battery-operated Christmas lights decorated the ladder and truck windows. Fire people stood on the back, tossing locally made saltwater taffy at the crowds. Mary chased pieces down and brought them to her mother to hold.

Christmas music played over speakers in the Gazebo in the center of town. The high school band was next with Esther's friend, Ferguson, playing the trombone. He was short, and she was sure that when the slide was out, he was going to tip over. The power company's truck had a massive blow up Snoopy and Woodstock on a Christmassy doghouse. Every float, car, or truck tossed candy, glow sticks, and saltwater taffy.

The bicycle rental company was one of Esther's favorites. The family that owned it was large. They always rode unicycles and did a little routine to the Christmas music that made Esther wish she was coordinated.

The Kids Club, the library, and almost every business in town had a float, car, or truck decorated and in the parade.

When it looked as if the parade was winding down, the final firetruck, the large ladder truck, blew its siren, announcing Santa Claus. It was usually

Darin from the chamber of commerce. He looked so much like Santa Claus that whenever Mary saw him in the grocery store or downtown, she regularly told him what she wanted for Christmas. He would go right along with the charade and ask her if her room was clean and if she was a good girl.

"Ho! Ho! Ho!" Santa Darin was perched on the ladder truck, waving like a beauty queen. Next to Darin, Grandma Mable looked like an angry elf, waving and shouting at kids to stay back from the fire engine.

No one listened. Kids were squealing and the entire crowd merged into the town square and surrounded the gazebo. Santa Darin's large elves—Burt, who owned the hardware store, and Dennis, who volunteered for everything in town—carried big bags into the Gazebo.

"Go, Grandma Mable!" Sophie yelled.

"Woot, Woot!" Nephi called.

Grandma Mable took charge of the chaos. She lined kids up in her bossy Grandma Mable way, she brought them to Santa one by one, and then waited while parents took pictures and collected their children. There must have been a hundred children lined up for Santa.

Mary was close to the head of the line, holding a torn piece of paper with words in pencil written and a Crayola Christmas tree. She had on her favorite Christmas sweater with the Grinch on the front, her unicorn hat, and sparkle boots.

Esther couldn't help but smile. As annoying as Mary was, Esther realized her heart was full of love for her. Mary was so excited she was hopping. Esther watched Papa J happily listening to her nonstop talk.

Finally, when it was Mary's turn, she climbed onto Santa Darin's lap and must have been so cute that the local newspaper photographer stepped to the front of the crowd and took her picture, along with Santa's and Grandma Mable's.

After the last child gave Santa his wish list, Santa Darin led the entire town in a round of carols, ending with "We Wish You a Merry Christmas."

As if on cue, the crowd quieted. Santa turned the tree off and then back on. Everyone cheered wildly.

"There are donuts and hot cider for everyone on the south side of the Gazebo," Grandma Mable announced.

"Ho! Ho! Ho!" Santa Darin Laughed. Esther watched Grandma Mable trying to slip through the crowd back to the family, with Santa Darin behind her. Santa Darin reached out and touched Grandma Mable's shoulder. She spun around, hands up ready for a fight. Esther couldn't hear what was being said, but Santa wiggled his brows like a lovesick puppy and tried to move closer to Grandma Mable.

"Sophie, look," Esther said.

"I think I just threw up in my mouth a little. Come on, Grandma Mable. Clock him one," Sophie said.

"I wish I could hear what he's saying."

"It would traumatize me."

Santa looked up, locked eyes with Esther, backed up, and slipped away into the crowd. Watching him go, Esther caught sight of Kol and Raini talking in the shadows. Raini was crying.

Ash was standing silently outside the group. He didn't notice her. He did see Kol. He moved toward Raini and Kol. The crowd closed around them.

"What if Kol is a part of what happened to Stanley?" Esther asked.

"I wouldn't even be surprised," Sophie said.

"I'll be right back." Esther had to get assertive to get through the people to where Kol and Raini were. "Excuse me. Can I get through?"

"Move!" Sophie finally barked. An older gentleman wearing a suit and tie pulled his chin in and folded his arms, refusing to move. By the time they got through, Kol, Ash, and Raini were gone.

"We need a murder board," Esther said.

"For Stanley? He's still with us," Sophie said.

"For Hazel and Stanley."

"I'll tell the others."

Bridget Merriweather walked home with the group, joining Esther, Sophie, and the rest in the garage behind Esther's house. It was their place to gather.

The James home was three stories in the front, with a basement apartment and garage in the back, where the property sloped toward the river. It was hidden in a circle of pines. The garage doors were old and wooden, as was the door to Grandma Mable's apartment. The door had a rounded portico protecting the mail and door from the rain.

Nephi opened the large garage door, and Parker pulled his vintage twenty-one window 1972 VW Van in. The van was perfect, but the group still tinkered to make it just that much better. Tonight was a cleaning night, or so they told their parents.

Without much chatter, the cold and tired group gathered. Parker opened the side door and pulled out the shop vac. Then he sat on a rolling cart.

Nephi opened the mini-fridge and passed Coke Zeroes and waters out. Sophie searched the tool bench until she came up with a bag of Doritos. Paisley and Bridget worked, lighting a fire in the wood-burning stove.

With a sharpie in hand, Esther waited until everyone gathered. They sat on coolers, crates, and lawn chairs around a freshly painted spot on the garage wall.

As if on cue, they were silent for a moment.

"As you know," Esther began, "Hazel died tragically, and the police decided it was an accident. I don't believe that. What do you all think?"

Esther wrote Hazel's name in the center of the wall and waited.

"You know what I think," Sophie said. "Kol or Draven did it on purpose. It was no accident. The mezzanine was updated just last year when they put the new shelves in. I can't imagine them not updating the railing."

"As soon as the book was found in your car," Parker said, "I knew we would have to sort this out. Whoever it is, is willing to lay the blame at your feet or any one of ours, I'm sure."

"Agreed," Nephi said. Bridget and Paisley nodded in agreement.

Grandma Mable came into the garage with her hair sticking up every which way, a run in her elf tights, and a flannel shirt covering the elf costume. No one noticed, but Esther. All they saw was the plate Grandma Mable carried with the gingerbread men and sugar cookies on it.

"Did you start without me?" Grandma Mable asked.

"Cookies!" Sophie exclaimed. Then she pulled back. "These look strange. This one is missing his leg. Did someone already take a bite out of him?"

"These are my cookie rejects. I froze the good ones and saved them for Christmas day."

"Whoa," Paisley said. "Epic Pinterest fail. Someone call the Island of Misfit toys; their cook has escaped."

"Not the gumdrop buttons!" Nephi laughed at his own joke.

"You're a monster!" Sophie pushed him.

"All right, kids, settle down," Esther said.

"Okay, Mum." Parker smiled at her.

Esther wrote Stanley's name next to Hazel's. "And even though Stanley is still with us, I think we need to look at the suspicious circumstances of his accident."

Paisley raised her hand, making Esther chuckle. "You're not in class."

Paisley smiled and put her hand down. "Who had a motive to take out both of those people? And how do we know it wasn't just an accident in both cases? I've been to the old bookstore a few times. In the past, they had the mezzanine roped off except for parties. It's an old building."

Esther studied Paisley before she answered her difficult question. "I see one thing that ties the two events together in a way that makes me think they aren't just coincidence. It's the box of inkwells, ink, and quills. Hazel found something in the box before Raini saw her fall from the balcony. On the balcony, someone might have pushed her outside the view of others."

"Who would want some old ink?" Bridget asked.

"That is the million-dollar question, isn't it?" Esther said. Off to the side of the patch of white paint on the wall she wrote "research uses of ink and value of ink and inkwells."

"Esther and I already talked to Ramona," Sophie said. "The one inkwell that was in the box and at the store was worth only a few thousand, according to her."

Bridget turned to see Sophie's face. "Yes, but that's according to the person who was selling it and who has a lot to lose. Would you go all out, over a piece worth a few thousand, and kill someone? No, I don't think so. Maybe she said it was only worth a few thousand, and it was worth more."

"She did say she felt bad about buying it from the other bookstore at such a deep discount," Esther said.

"She didn't feel bad enough to give the seller more money, did she?" Nephi asked.

After making three columns with her marker, Esther wrote the words "Possible Motive" at the top of the first column, then "Research Needed" on the next column, and "Who will do the research," on the last column.

"Put money under motive," Sophie said. "Then under 'Research Needed' put *inkwells* and *rare books*. Then put me down as the person doing the research. I am going to get online tonight and google vintage inkwells, ink bottles, and the cost or last sale of the missing list of items."

"Bring me up to speed," Grandma Mable said.

"Well, you already know we are suspicious of both Hazel's death and Stanley's accident, and that someone planted one of the stolen items in the Jeep. And you know that a book, inkwells, and ink are missing, and maybe more." Esther pointed at Stanley's and Hazel's names on the wall, and then the research list with Sophie's name, since she was volunteering to research the ink, inkwells, and rare books.

"Motive. Always look for the motive," Grandma Mable said. She pulled up a lawn chair. "I say we go through the list of people we know are attached to both these incidents."

Esther wrote Ramona on the wall. "Ramona bought the box Hazel was searching through, and Ramona knows books, and the worth of the other items. She lost her competitor when the accident happened. Honestly, my gut says she is innocent, but the facts are she would know how to profit from any of the items."

"Why not just sell them instead of going through this charade?" Grandma Mable asked.

"Good question," Paisley said.

"And I didn't see any animosity between her and Stanley," Esther said.

"Who else is attached to both events?" Grandma Mable asked.

Esther put both names off to the side, leaving room to write. "Raini. But it isn't her. She is caring for her dying mother."

"She seems sweet and weak but could need money because she's the only child of a cancer patient. Could that be the motive?" Bridget asked.

"Harsh!" Nephi said.

"Just because she's a girl, doesn't mean she can't make some serious mistakes. Just look at me," Paisley said.

"What about you?" Nephi asked.

She gave Nephi one of her glorious smiles and a buddy push.

"Okay, you two. I'm one tired elf. Any other ideas?" Grandma Mable said.

"Draven 'Coldhearted' Kane," Sophie said.

"What's his motive?" Mable asked.

"Money," Esther answered.

"Money is a solid motive. Does he need money or have money? Give me your thoughts."

Esther looked at Grandma Mable, chewed her lip, and thought for a moment. "I can't get this picture out of my mind. Stanley under the bookshelves, and Draven telling us to be careful of damaging the books. The books were more important than Stanley."

"That's cold," Bridget said.

Grandma Mable nodded in agreement.

Esther wrote Draven Kane's name down. "His alibi for the incident didn't hold up either. He said he was fixing the toilet at the tiny house Alvah's rents from them. It fell apart when police questioned Alvah, who said he was at her house for far less pure reasons."

One of Grandma Mable's brows rose. "If you lie about one thing, I won't usually trust you on anything else, unless you're a cute seven-year-old in a unicorn onesie."

"No one can resist Mary," Paisley laughed. "She didn't do it."

"What about Kol?" Sophie asked.

"What's his motive?" Grandma Mable asked.

The group was silent until Sophie stood and wrote his name down.

"Mean. His motive is being as mean as a snake," Sophie said. "And he likes Raini. He talked about her working because she needed money."

"We missed one," Esther said. She took the marker and wrote *Ash* on the wall.

"What motive would he possibly have?" Grandma Mable asked.

Esther turned and looked at the group. "Money. We don't know anything about him. We don't know how he bought the cottage and bakery or if he is deep in debt. Besides, I know I am not supposed to judge, but he has a past, a record of murder of some kind."

"I know exactly why he was in prison, and if you ask him, he might tell you too. Which takes us back to the big question. What is his motive?" Grandma Mable asked.

"Money? Revenge?" Esther asked.

"Did he live here before? Was he in prison in Oregon? How much money would entice a man who can afford to buy a home and a business? How do either of these incidents get someone money? We need to do research. The kind of deep googling you girls do best. Now! Let's eat these cookies and all get to bed. It's late. I am looking forward to sleeping in."

Esther stretched, yawned, and put her lawn chair away while Parker swept out the van. Sophie put her cooler chair and Doritos away. Paisley stirred the fire and made sure it was out.

"Sleepover?" Sophie asked.

"Of course," Esther said.

"I will text my parental units."

The James house was quiet. Nephi had fallen asleep in front of a movie. Esther and Sophie turned all the lights off and snuck upstairs to Esther's room.

They raised the trundle and pulled a pillow out of the closet for Sophie. Once Miss Molly was purring in her lap, Esther began scrolling on her phone while Sophie used her laptop.

"Look at this." Esther held her phone up to show Sophie a photo of an inkwell.

"What is it?" Sophie asked.

"If Ash's inkwell is like this inkwell, it's solid and very pure or the purest gold, valued at almost twenty thousand just for the gold. The fact that it is almost two hundred years old makes it worth more, I would imagine. Especially if they have the history of the piece."

"But why kill for it? He already has one?"

"I don't know why," Esther said.

"We're missing something." Sophie threw herself back onto the bed. "We need sleep."

"Sleep is for the weak," Esther chuckled.

"I thought that was the wise."

"There is something nagging me about all of this. A memory. I can't quite put it together." Esther took Miss Molly and climbed into bed.

"Tomorrow..." Sophie trailed off.

13

I t was three-thirty in the morning when Esther sat straight up in bed, pulling her hair out from underneath Miss Molly. She had been dreaming about something that felt so real it terrified her.

Miss Molly meowed in protest, but Esther didn't hear her. She could still see the dream unfold.

Her parents were arguing. Someone had died, but she couldn't remember who. It wasn't someone she knew. In the dream, her father said, "The man next door didn't do it." And her mother stood, stoic, and said, "The neighbor did it." But what he did, Esther couldn't remember. The dream, like a lost memory, was swimming just out of sight, like the fish that got away.

She lay back down and tried to remember. Miss Molly joined her on the pillow. When the morning sun woke her, she was having the same dream. Unable to go back to sleep, she began google-stalking Ash Corradao.

All her social media searches dead ended. Then she tried a general Google search. A news story popped up with the same last name, but the boy's first name was Ashley.

Ashley Corradao had been tried as an adult for driving drunk and killing a woman and her two daughters, ages one and nine. The article said he entered into a plea agreement that would let him out in fifteen years on good behavior if he was granted parole. The woman's husband was quoted three times in the article. He said he was angry and didn't believe Ash should ever get out. He said if his daughters didn't get lives, then neither should Ash.

In the photos, Ash didn't have the muscle he had now. He did have hair. It hung in long hanks over his eyes, and he tried unsuccessfully to hide his face in the photo. He was tattoo free and actually, very handsome, in Esther's opinion. He had the same large, dark eyes.

He must have lifted weights while he was in prison. She knew that prisoners did homemade tattoos, but one of his tattoos on his upper arm looked almost tribal and complicated.

She continued the search and found a small article. It announced his release after serving his full sentence. The husband and father of the victims was quoted in the article and still sounded bitter and angry. There was something in the article that made Esther read it twice. Then she realized the article was in the Salt Lake Tribune's online edition. Ash might have served his time in the same prison her father was in and at the same time.

"Sophie," Esther whispered and touched her.

"What?"

"Look at this."

Sophie rolled over, her long, black hair completely knotted over her face. She pushed it aside, reached for her glasses on the desk, put them on, and took Esther's phone.

Sophie sat up. "This is why Ash was in for murder? Sounds like manslaughter to me. You know, not premeditated."

"Look closer," Esther said.

"It's too early." Sophie held her hair back with her right hand and held the phone up with her left.

Esther studied her face. Sophie's eyes were narrowed and drawn together. She mouthed the words as she reread the article. Then in exasperation, she rolled her eyes.

"Tell me," Sophie begged.

"Nope."

"Give me a hint."

"Check the name of the digital media service featuring the article," Esther said.

"Shut the front door! He could have been in prison with your dad. How many prisons are there in Utah?" Sophie scrolled back and forth. "And he was there at the same time!"

"Yup. I don't know what it means or if it is merely a coincidence. But you also know what Madison Merriweather and my mother both say. 'There is no such thing as coincidence. And real life is better than any book in the world.'"

"Wait. Hold the biscuits." Sophie typed rapidly on Esther's phone, both thumbs going at lightning speed.

Esther put her hand over her mouth, trying not to giggle. Sophie was concentrating so much that her tongue was sticking out of her mouth sideways, as it used to in elementary school when she took tests.

"Okay. There are two prisons currently operating in the state of Utah. The one your father is in by Salt Lake and one further south. There is a fifty-fifty chance they were in the slammer together."

Esther couldn't help herself. She smiled. "The slammer? Okay... There is someone else I want to look up before I video-call Dad to confirm he knows Ashley or Ash."

"Who's that?" Sophie asked.

"My bio-grandfather who just passed away."

"Okay, but before you go down that Google trail, we have to be at work in one hour, and I am going to starve to death any minute," Sophie said.

"Sorry, Miss Molly, you have to get down. I am going to feed you and find something for us," Esther said.

Miss Molly meowed and headed downstairs, looking for cat food.

14

—·—

T he girls were the last to leave the bookstore again. Ramona had gone to the hospital with a home-cooked meal for Desdemona. All the girls had to do was take the cash from the drawer, put it in a banker's bag, and take the bag up to the rare books room and leave it in her office.

"Do you think the guys are still here? We could ask Ash if he was in prison with your bio-dad," Sophie said.

Using a nasal voice, Esther put her nose high in the air and looked every bit a snob as she's ever known. "Oh, right? I say, Ash. I hear you were in lockup with my pop. Is that right?"

Sophie snickered. "Okay. Not the best plan."

"You just want Nephi to still be in the bakery." Esther smiled while she turned the lock on the inside of the front door and pulled it closed behind them.

Sophie pointed up at Esther. "Don't even tease. He is in love with Paisley. And besides, he is like a brother to me."

"Okay. I'll stop teasing you."

"I will believe that when it happens."

The lights were still on inside the bakery, but the sign was off. Ash was behind the counter doing something in a ledger. Parker and Nephi were putting their coats on. Bubba had his on and was sitting by the door.

Esther knocked softly on the paned windows. Parker saw her and beamed while he opened the door.

"Goodnight, Ash," Parker called over his shoulder.

Nephi and Bubba followed his lead. "Goodnight!"

Parker gave Esther a warm hug.

"Are you coming over tonight? I have some news for the murder wall," Esther said.

"I can't tonight. You'll never guess who arrived this morning all the way from Britain." Parker smiled, and his eyes twinkled. Esther couldn't remember the last time she had seen him this happy.

"Your Grandfather?"

"Yes! Grandad Stuart."

"Do I call him Lord Stuart?" Esther asked.

"I don't know. That's a good question." Parker shrugged. "I guess you could ask him. Here he is now."

Doctor Stuart, Parker's father, pulled in, driving a black SUV. Parker ran to the passenger door, pulled it open, and a man that looked to be Grandma Mable's age got out of the car.

"Parker!" His grandfather hugged Parker fiercely. He was a few inches taller than Parker. And even though he was older, he looked like a cheerful middle-aged man with salt-and-pepper hair, until she got close enough to see smile lines from years of laughter permanently showing the world he had a happy disposition.

"Grandad, this is Esther."

"Hello... Lord Stuart?" Esther said. Parker's grandfather chuckled.

"Esther. I have heard all about you for hours on end. This boy is totally smitten," Lord Stuart said.

Parker's face was positively red, and now Nephi was laughing.

"Father," Parker said, "can Esther and our friends come to help us decorate the Christmas tree tonight?"

"Oh, I don't know. It's already six o'clock," Dr. Stuart said.

"Come now. I'm only here for a short time. I say we wassail it up and burn the midnight oil," Lord Stuart said. He looked very much like Parker, with graying hair and a definite twinkle in his brown eyes.

The back window of the SUV rolled down, and Paisley leaned out. "Parker, get in! We're picking up pizza, and it's going to get cold."

"Pizza?" Nephi asked.

Paisley smiled like a movie star, and Esther watched Nephi melt.

"Do you want to come?" Paisley asked.

Nephi looked over his shoulder at his beat-up truck and said, "I'll meet you there. I want to go home and take a shower."

"Bring your mum," Paisley said.

Nephi shrugged. "I'll ask. She might be watching Mary."

"Bring Mary too," Lord Stuart said.

"You don't know what you're asking for," Nephi said.

"The more the merrier," Lord Stuart said.

"May I join you?" Sophie asked.

Paisley laughed musically. "Sophie! You don't need to ask. I better call Bridget and Madison, and the Pizza Ship to Shore Restaurant and order more food. We are going to need more pizza."

The doors to the SUV closed, and Parker's father drove away from the bookstore's parking lot.

Esther waved, but Parker didn't notice. He was leaning over the front seat, joyfully smiling and chatting away.

"Let's get home and change. Would your parents want to go?" Esther asked.

"I'm sure they'd rather splice a gene. I was going to tell you. We are flying to Hawaii the day after Christmas for the remainder of Christmas vacation," Sophie said.

"Your grandmother is going to be so happy to see you."

"We have to go. She has another new boyfriend, and she says this one is a keeper."

"He might be." Esther shrugged. She threw her book bag in the back seat of the Jeep, got in, and turned the key, starting the motor.

"And pigs can fly to their own luau."

Papa J was working, but Esther's mother, Grandma Mable, and Mary wanted to go to the Stuarts and help decorate their tree.

Esther pulled her fisherman's sweater over her head, making her hair emerge from the neck like a ball of frizzy brown curls with auburn streaks.

"Can I borrow a sweater?" Sophie asked.

"Sure." Esther spritzed the frizz with shine spray and ran her fingers through it, catching them in a large tangle. Sophie disappeared down the hall into Mary's room and came back with a child-size black sweater with glitter around the neck.

"Do you think she'll mind?" Sophie asked.

"No. That's last year's sweater. I wish mom and Mary didn't have to come," Esther said.

"Why? My family won't, and I wish they would come," Sophie said.

Esther rolled her eyes. "No one can predict Mary, and how does a Lord respond to a child who thinks she is a unicorn?"

"That was last week. This week, we are mermaids."

"I'm glad one of us can track her movements. You don't suppose she'll wear those shells over her shirt again?"

"They're better than the unicorn onesie," Sophie said.

"Girls! Are you ready?" Esther's mother called from downstairs.

Esther and Sophie rushed down the stairs.

"I'll take my own car, Mom," Esther said.

"Nephi already left. Can't we ride together as a family in my new car?"

"Maybe next time," Esther said. She and Sophie grabbed their matching black coats and beanies from the closet and went out the door before she could stop them.

Parker and Paisley lived with their parents in the Captain's Cove Mansion, a local landmark. Its wrought-iron fence was ornate, but not as ornate as the gingerbread gables recently repainted white on white under the cedar-shingled roof of the eleven thousand square foot Victorian.

Esther parked down the street so her mother could park in the driveway. The front gate squeaked, making General Cornwallis, Parker's dog, go wild behind the front door. The motion-sensor lights turned on, and Parker opened one of the double doors, smiling and holding the family's large Terrier Doodle mixed-breed dog.

"Quiet, Cornwallis," Parker said to no avail.

The girls ascended the stone steps to the wraparound porch. Esther reached out, and Cornwallis slobbered all over her hand. She scratched behind his ears, and he tried to jump on her.

"Down, boy! Down!" Parker smiled and rolled his eyes. The dog moved to Sophie, who spoke baby talk to him while scratching behind his ears. Parker turned around and led them through the grand entryway with its sweeping staircase and to the double doors on the left.

The doors were open, and Christmas music was playing in one of Esther's favorite rooms in all the world, the Stuarts' study. The dark wood room with red oriental rugs was almost surrounded by shelves of books. The only spot that didn't have books was the river rock fireplace, which was burning brightly under a mantle of holly bows and flickering candles of various heights.

A spiral staircase wound up to the mezzanine, which surrounded the room with a second story of books and a stained-glass window and seating area. The iron railing around the mezzanine was strung with flickering Christmas lights.

Mrs. Stuart was her usual gracious self and gathered Esther into a welcoming hug.

Parker brought his grandfather over to the group. "Grandad, I would like to introduce you to Esther's mother, Grace James; her sister, Mary; and her Grandmother, Mable."

Then Esther saw something quite unexpected and yet something that happened frequently. Lord Stuart took one look at her redheaded Grandma Mable and was speechless.

Sophie gently elbowed her and rolled her eyes. "Here we go again."

Completely ignoring her mother and sister, he bowed to her grandmother. "I have heard so much about you. It is so lovely to finally meet you all."

"Kneel, king." Mary raised her favorite sparkle wand.

Her mother stepped between Mary and Lord Stuart. "Excuse her. She's decided she is a queen."

Lord Stuart's smile charmed Esther. "Are you a queen often?"

"When she isn't a mermaid or a unicorn," Grandma Mable said.

Lord Stuart was once again mesmerized by Grandma Mable. "May I offer you wassail?"

He walked away with Grandma Mable. Esther couldn't hear what they were talking about over the music, but he was laughing loudly, and Grandma Mable broke from her usual dry wit and deadpan face and laughed alongside him.

"Parker?" her mother asked.

"Yes?"

"I thought we should bring something for your tree." She held up a small box.

"When did you do this?" Esther asked.

"Today."

"What is it?"

"You'll see," her mother said.

Esther looked at her mother, who smiled back at her.

Her mother looked at Esther and then back at Parker. "Your family has become a part of our family. At the James house, we have a tradition. Every Christmas we make ornaments for our tree. One year it was heavy salt clay—too heavy as it turned out. Another year it was pinecone and pretzel reindeer. Unfortunately, Mary ate their legs last year. I thought this one might be a good start for your tree, if you would like to join us to make ornaments this year."

"I would be honored." Parker put his arm around Esther. "We love your family."

"Go ahead. Open it!" Mary exclaimed.

"Now?" Parker asked.

"Your queen demands it," Mary said.

"All right." Parker untied the red yarn that held the box together and opened it.

Esther felt her heart drop and heat color her face. "Mom, really? He doesn't want—"

Parker interrupted her by hugging her. "I love it." He walked to the tree with Esther on his heels.

"You don't have to hang it up," Esther said.

"When did you make it?"

"I was eight."

"It's perfect." Parker hung up the paper and dental-floss ornament that was in the shape of a snowman front and center on the family's tall tree.

Esther's mother had a bag with her. She found Parker's mom, who helped her pull a folding table and chairs into the room and then cover the table with a cloth. Paisley joined them, and soon Esther realized her mother had brought their homemade ornaments for the year to the party.

Esther's mother held up a clear plastic ornament. "I printed photos from our Thanksgiving dinner. I think I have one of everyone, including Marion, who isn't here. These clear plastic ornaments open like this." She pulled the silver top out of the ornament and pulled the plastic into two pieces so the front and back were separated.

"I've brought various supplies, including glitter," Esther's mom said.

"Nephi, come help me," Paisley said.

"I'll find all the photos of myself."

"I also have pizza in the kitchen and Christmas cookies. Everyone, help yourself," Parker's mom said over the noise.

Esther loved moments like these, when she felt normal, as though nothing in the world could shatter the magic of friendship and Christmas all at the same time. She watched Lord Stuart sit by the fire and talk animatedly to Grandma Mable, who was using her silent interrogation tactic. She used it on Esther and Nephi regularly. She didn't say a thing. She just nodded. Meanwhile, her victims found themselves babbling or, worse, telling her their life stories, including the reason she should punish them or whatever rules they'd broken.

The doors opened, and Madison Merriweather, world-famous, best-selling author, dressed in her traditional black with her black hair sleeked into a bun, took center stage in the room, with Bridget trying to hide behind her.

Arms flung wide, she said, "Darlings! Merry Christmas!"

The tree was covered top to bottom. Dr. Stuart was on a tall ladder. Her mother was on the mezzanine, and Mrs. Stuart was directing the production with the help of Madison Merriweather.

Interestingly, Grandma Mable and Lord Stuart were still talking on the couch, only they had closed most of the distance between them. Grandma Mable laughed musically, and Esther's jaw dropped.

"Did you hear that?" Esther asked.

"I can't believe what I am seeing," Sophie said.

"They have been talking nonstop for three hours."

"Where is Mary?" Sophie asked.

"Stringing popcorn for the mantle with Paisley."

"Yum. Maybe I should help them," Sophie said.

While Esther watched Sophie, Parker snuck up behind her, put his arms around her waist, and said, "This is the best Christmas I can remember."

"It isn't Christmas yet," Esther said.

"Isn't it?" Parker smiled.

15

— • —

Sophie had gone home; the house was dark and quiet. The only sound was Miss Molly purring. Esther sat cross-legged on her chenille bedspread, with only the light of her laptop in the room. She had lost all track of time.

She found the obituary for her bio-grandfather who had passed away. It took some looking. She had to search obituaries for everyone with the last name of Day born between 1920 and 1950, which was only a guess. When she found him, she was shocked. He was older than she expected. She knew her grandmother had died years ago, but she didn't realize that she still had a grandfather. He was in his late 90s when he passed away.

She finally found him by searching her father's full name, Morgan David Day, and the word obituary. The photo was old.

Richard Alfred Day looked about twenty in the photo and was in a uniform from the war. He was a survivor of D-Day on Normandy Beach. He went on to earn his fortune as an entrepreneur and was later a CEO and owner of a pharmaceutical conglomerate that made things like insulin and drugs to treat cancer patients. He made the bulk of his fortune by age fifty and then diversified, thereby expanding his fortune. Then, from what Esther could see through her multiple searches, he left the limelight and faded from public view. The obituary touted his many successes, but Esther noticed that despite his fortune, it didn't say anything like in lieu of flowers donate to his favorite charity. It didn't list any great works of service or any contributions to charitable projects.

He had died in Fairfax County, Virginia. She had been able to locate an address for him and used Google Street View to walk around his palatial country estate, complete with a private driving range and golf carts parked in the circular drive the day Google photographed the property.

The most interesting part of the obituary was the last paragraph.

"Richard Alfred Day is survived by his two sons, Mustang Dee Day of Fairfax County, and David Morgan Day. It didn't say anything else about her father. There were no photos of Mustang in the obituary.

Like his father, Mustang was not on social media, no matter how deep she dug. She did, however, find him in an article listing his name as a graduate of Yale Law School. Guessing that he probably went straight from his high school or private school to Yale, Esther estimated his age at approximately fifteen years older than her father, or fifty-five. She wondered if they had different mothers. She couldn't find any other articles about Mustang other than the obituary, not even an online photo posted by someone else.

She put all the links in a note and emailed her findings to Sophie.

Feeling guilty for not spending more energy researching the inkwell and missing quills, she checked the time. It was one-thirty in the morning. She wasn't tired. She was spun. Her mind was reeling. Why had her father never mentioned her grandfather? Were they close?

She didn't know a thing about her grandmother. She wanted desperately to begin a new search, her curious mind spinning, when she heard something outside her open window.

The curtains were open. After all, she was on the third floor, without another house between her and the sea. She had a private view of the ocean, and no one could look through her window at night unless they climbed the outside tree or ivy.

She crept over to the window. The sound was a squeak, squeak, of a rusty wheel. In the spotlight of a streetlamp, she saw a man in dark clothes, pulling a child's wagon down the road. A dog with a Santa hat walked next to him. He stopped at the neighbor's recycling can, opened the lid, and she heard him going through the garbage, pulling out cans. In Oregon, there was a ten-cent deposit on all bottles and cans. Recycling cans could make someone enough money for a meal if they filled a few bags.

Esther's family drank a lot of diet coke. When he got to their cans, the process took several minutes. Meanwhile, it started to rain lightly. The man filled a garbage bag—he must have brought it with him—and piled it on top of the other two in his wagon. He picked one more bag up with his free hand and continued down the road.

Miss Molly jumped onto her desk and meowed at her. Esther pulled the window down so the rain wouldn't get in on her laptop, set her alarm for eight in the morning, and crawled into bed to sleep.

And yet, she was awake and thinking for almost another hour. Why hadn't her mother told her about her father's family? Why hadn't her father said anything?

Maybe I would have liked my grandfather. Now I'll never know.

She didn't know anything about golf. He was smart. Was she like him? He didn't look very nice.

When she did sleep, she dreamed she was lost inside in her grandfather's large Fairfax County house, running down wood-paneled hallway after hallway, through room after room, not finding any doors for her escape. The house didn't have any windows.

16

— : —

During school, Esther and Sophie usually spent several hours a day in their favorite sanctuary, the Oceanside High library, with Ms. Cynommon Priest, the librarian. They tried to time their classes together so that if the library was slow, they could use the period for study, but today they had a mess to clean up.

The school required all students to return their library books before Christmas break so an inventory could be taken on lost or missing items and because, in their small beach town, kids moved. Many families couldn't pay their rent and were evicted during the harsh winter months. Hotels and restaurants slowed down and jobs went away. That meant that when students returned after Christmas break, inevitably twenty or more kids would have moved out of town, permanently, along with the books they had checked out before the holidays. To avoid losing that many books annually, they used the inventory as a reason to round up the student's books.

The double doors to the library opened, and Ferguson, the freshman volunteer that Esther and Sophie had taken under their wings, pushed a cart of books in.

"I collected these from students during lunch. I'll collect books again when the last bell rings," Ferguson said.

"Great idea, Ferg," Sophie said.

They unloaded the cart onto a reading table covered with books waiting to be shelved.

"I'm going back out to beg for books," Ferguson said.

"Do you need my Taser?" Sophie asked. Ferguson turned and grinned broadly.

"No weapons in school, Sophie! If you have one, surrender it now," Ms. Priest called from her office.

Ferguson laughed and pushed the cart out into the hall.

"I don't know how she does that," Sophie said. "She hears everything. She must be part bat."

"I heard that," Ms. Priest announced from her desk.

"Do you think we can get this mess cleared before work?" Esther asked, sorting books into piles.

"There are only four more days before Christmas break. We need at least another week," Sophie said.

"Do you have any tests this week?" Esther asked.

"Nope."

"Don't forget our assignments in lit. We have an essay and a review of the research paper due one day after we return."

"What did you decide to review?" Sophie asked.

"Since we are allowed to review any research we want, I decided to review the forensic science of carbon dating ink and carbon dating as it relates to important historical papyri and documents."

One of Sophie's eyebrows rose, and she folded her arms. "Picked something easy, didn't you?"

"The assignment is to make sure we know how to cite the research and collect credible sources. After the paper goes in, we also have to write a news article using AP style."

"Are you sure you want to write about something so exciting as ink?"

"Oh, yeah. Well, attempted murder or even Hazel's murder would make for some interesting reading." Esther smiled.

"Our police force is so happy to make everything an accident and to avoid murder. Your little article could either get you into trouble with them or give them a reason to go after you again."

Ms. Priest came out of her office and picked up a pile of books. "How is it going?"

Esther waved a hand like a game show host across the table. "This is the easy part. Next, we make them all fit on the shelves in order."

Ms. Priest smiled, but then her brows knit, and she put her books down and went to the double library doors and looked through the glass windows. The doors led to the hall. A man passed by the windows too fast for Esther to see who he was. Then the coin dropped. *Blue shirt. Police Officer.*

Esther and Sophie watched with Ms. Priest, who held the door open so they could all peek out. A uniformed officer joined Chief Lampii and the new detective at a locker just down the hall. Principal Brocklehurst watched as Bob, the janitor, cut off the lock.

"Whose locker is that?" Sophie whispered.

Esther shook her head back and forth and shrugged. She had no idea.

The chief opened the locker door. In no time at all, he pulled out an Egyptian inkwell and three bottles of ink.

Sophie's sharp intake of breath was loud enough to make the chief look up at them. They all jumped and stepped back inside the library, holding their breath, waiting, hoping that even though he looked right at them, he hadn't seen them.

Of course he had.

The door to the library opened so quickly it almost hit Ms. Priest, who caught it just in time. Chief Lampii opened it the rest of the way while they stepped back.

"How do you girls always get into the middle of a mess like this?" Chief Lampii asked.

"We don't know what you mean," Ms. Priest said. Esther knew she was trying to be protective, but he wasn't buying it.

"Don't give me that. Which one of you knew that this inkwell was in Raini's locker? Hmm?"

Esther's eyes grew wide. Her heart was beating so hard she could hear blood rushing in her ears. "It's a setup, Chief. Just like I was set up."

"Oh, yeah? Well, what would the point be in setting up a schoolgirl like Raini?" the chief asked. "Why would anyone ever bother with her? Maybe Raini and Kol need money?"

"Biscuits!" Sophie exclaimed. "Everyone in this tiny town needs money, Chief."

"Sophia Ito, watch your tone," Chief Lampii said.

"Oh, come on, Chief! Does Raini strike you as a stone-cold murderer?" Sophie asked.

Esther nodded.

The chief looked back and forth between them, once, twice, and then deflated. "This is an ongoing investigation. That means you ladies stay away from the press and don't go getting yourselves all messed up in the middle of it. You got me?"

He pointed at Esther, then Sophie, and back to Esther, looking over the top of his aviators.

"Chief. You think Hazel was murdered, don't you?" Esther said.

"Esther James, I could still haul you in on that book we found in your car."

Esther stepped back.

The chief took off his aviators and rubbed his eyes. "Exactly. No one is arresting Raini. The detective is going down to the office to do her job and talk to her. That's all."

Sophie pushed past the chief and ran down the hall at an impressive speed.

Bob yelled, "Hey! No running in the hall." But she was gone before he started the sentence.

The chief sighed, gritted his teeth, hunched his shoulders, and marched off after Sophie.

"Come on," Esther whispered.

"I wouldn't miss this for the world," Ms. Priest said.

They walked quietly behind the chief, who turned the corner and went left, the same direction Sophie had gone.

"Sophia Ito!" the chief barked. "You stop right now!"

Esther sprang ahead, and she and Ms. Priest turned the corner just in time to see Sophie hand Raini one dollar and make a call on her phone.

She shrugged shoulders and turned her nose up at the chief. "Hello, Charles? This is Sophie. Yes, Ito. We have an emergency at the school. Your new client, Raini, needs you."

"Sophia Ito," Chief Lampii said, "I ought to arrest you for interfering in a police investigation!"

"She has the right to remain silent, Chief, and she has the right to hire an attorney should she want one. Charles is on his way."

"Woot! Woot!" Esther had both hands in the air when the chief spun on his heels.

"I may not be able to arrest you, Esther James, but I sure as tooting can order your father to ground you! Now, Raini. Follow me into the office."

Raini held onto her dollar and, looking at both girls through wide, watery eyes over a quivering lip, followed the chief into the principal's office where Detective Garcia-Smith and the officer were meeting with the Principal Brocklehurst. He closed the door.

Then they heard Desdemona Brocklehurst's muffled voice. The door opened back up, and she pointed to the school exit. "If you feel the need to interrogate a child, do it in your own station, not my school."

The chief shook his head, waved for the detective and uniformed officer, who winked at Esther, to follow him.

"Chief!" the detective said. "She is interfering with our investigation."

"We're going, Garcia-Smith!" the chief said.

Garcia-Smith and the officer trotted behind the chief and out the school door.

Raini watched them go, wide eyed, and still holding her dollar bill.

Principal Brocklehurst's cell phone vibrated. She answered it. "Ramona? I'll be right there." She looked at the girls.

"Esther, Sophie, would you mind running the bookstore after school so Alvah can go home?" Miss Brocklehurst looked from girl to girl. "Stanley is awake."

The winter sky was already black at six o'clock. Sophie locked the door and turned the sign from open to closed. Esther counted the money into piles the way Ramona had trained her, wrote the total on a piece of paper, and zipped the cash and her note in a blue banker's bag.

She helped Sophie turn off the gas fireplace, Christmas tree, and lights. One light was on. It was in the rare books room.

Esther and Sophie stood at the bottom of the stairs, gazing up. Then they looked at each other.

"You know I hate breaking rules. It makes me sick," Esther said.

"Letting someone get away with murder makes me sick," Sophie said.

Wordlessly, they looked back up the stairs before climbing them. Esther followed Sophie into Ramona's office. Her computer was a desktop. The laptop from the rare books room had been left unplugged and put on the top of a small bookshelf.

Esther used her height to pull it down and carry it out. She and Sophie sat on the floor. Esther plugged in the computer and handed it to the expert, Sophie.

"It isn't password protected." Sophie smiled and rubbed her hands together.

"What? Can you do that? Have a computer without a password?" Esther asked.

"My grandmother does. It's an old person thing. She is always losing hers."

"Where should we start?"

"The search history. It won't show us who searched, but it will show what websites they've been to." Sophie rapidly opened the browser and pulled up the history.

"This is interesting," Sophie said.

"What is it?"

"It's a website for getting valuable books appraised and selling them online."

"How will we know if he asked to have any books appraised?" Esther asked.

"Simple, the browser he uses saves passwords. Old people love to make it easy. All I have to do is open the webpage, click on login..."

The login username and password auto-populated.

"Seriously? Please don't let me get this old," Esther said.

"Never fear. Your computer ninja will have your back." Sophie continued working rapidly.

"There it is!" Sophie hissed. She turned the screen so Esther could see.

The page clearly listed Stanley as the seller. There were ten valuable documents and some books.

"What if Stanley is selling Ramona's inventory without her permission or knowledge? There are a lot of books in this room. But he doesn't seem like the kind of person that would steal from his sister." Sophie pushed her glasses up and rubbed her eyes.

"How much does it all come to?" Esther asked.

Together they added it up in their head.

"One hundred and fifty thousand dollars. Jinx," they both said.

Sophie whistled. "Sherlock, I believe we have a motive, money. Lots of money."

"Yes, but we know the bookshelves were sabotaged. Why would the person getting lots of money try to kill himself by standing under bookshelves that they plan to push over? It doesn't make sense."

Esther chewed on her fingernail, thinking. "What if Stanley isn't the person getting the money? What if someone is using him? Look at his rating. He has a ninety-nine percent rating. Let's check his sales and purchase history."

Within a minute, Sophie had printed both the sales and the purchase histories out. Esther collected them from the printer.

"These go back more than a year," Esther said. "Look, there are sales from before Hazel was killed."

"So why open his own account at that time? Why not just work with his sister? What changed a little over a year ago?" Sophie asked.

Esther pointed at a book on the list "This is interesting. He purchased several books from the 1800s. Everything here dates from the same year as the book printed during the civil war. Look how many ink bottles he's purchased."

"Give me the name of one of the books he bought," Sophie said.

Esther listed three. Sophie only found one on the shelves. She brought it back to Esther.

"This book is in really bad shape." Sophie opened it and turned the pages all the way through.

Esther closed her eyes. "I keep remembering something from my childhood. Something to do with a neighbor. No. Something Dad and Mom argued about." She rubbed her forehead. "What was it?" And then she remembered. The memory hit her like white hot lightening, and all the pieces fell into place. "Give me the book."

Sophie handed the brown book to her. Esther turned to the back and ran her finger down what was left of a page expertly cut out of the back of the book.

"What?" Sophie asked.

"I am sure this was a blank page. This book is small, five by eight maybe. Give me the list of things he is selling." Esther looked back and forth at the pages of sales and purchases. "Look at the dates, Sophie. I think I know exactly what the motive is. But now we have a real problem."

"What do you mean? That's great. Case closed, right?" Sophie said.

"How do we explain how we got this information? What do we do? I can just see it now." Esther made a silly face, batted her eyelashes, and said, "Hey, Chief, I hacked the company computer and illegally used someone else's login. But that's okay because I know why someone tried to kill Stanley. No, I don't know who did it. But that's okay, right?"

"Well, crepes." Sophie sat back against the wall and closed her eyes.

"Grandma Mable always says follow the money. If there is an account, then the money gets deposited somewhere. Look at his profile on the website. Does the money go to a bank account or a credit card? Maybe there is a way to see how much money he's made, like a list of deposits emailed to him."

Sophie's fingers flew. She stopped, thought, and then rapidly entered more information. Click, click, and then she smiled. "You're never going to believe whose name is on the credit card he is using."

"Spill. Don't make me guess," Esther said.

"Alvah's. Surprised?" Sophie wiggled her brows and smiled smugly.

"No! Let me see."

Sophie turned the screen and pointed to Alvah's name as the name listed on the credit card in his profile.

"That's how he buys things. How does he accept payments? Does it go through the website or, like eBay, does it run through PayPal?" Esther asked.

"There are seller reviews. I guess we could buy something cheap and see if he uses PayPal."

"We couldn't afford anything on this list."

"So we are back to the original questions. If Stanley is buying and selling books online, he is profiting, so why kill Hazel and throw himself under the shelves? And is he working with Alvah, or is he just using her card? What if she is using him? Why would she try to kill the person she is using?" Sophie sighed.

"We know Alvah was in the store when Hazel died and had the opportunity to push her. Either Stanley stole Alvah's card or maybe she gave it to him voluntarily. They could be working together. It still doesn't tell us why the shelves were knocked over on Stanley. We're missing some pieces."

"Oh, biscuits! Did you hear that?" Sophie asked.

"What?"

"I heard a car door slam."

"Double biscuits! Go. Go!" Esther began frantically gathering everything they had printed and folding it up small enough to stick in the back of her jeans under her shirt.

Sophie quickly put the computers and hardware back where they found them.

"Look." Sophie held up a small flash drive attached to her house key on a key ring. She slowly smiled. Then it slipped from her sweaty hands to the floor. She took a step to pick up the key ring, but she accidentally kicked it with her foot, sending it sliding across the floor and under a bookshelf. After dropping to her knees, she put her thin fingers under the shelf, trying desperately to get to the key.

It was quiet enough that Esther heard someone walking on the gravel. She ran through the room, turned off the lights, and flew down the stairs.

Esther ran to the front door, tried to slow her breathing, put on her coat, and then opened the door when Ramona was about to unlock it.

17

—:—

Ramona's usually perfectly coiffed hair was slightly disheveled. Strands had fallen from her scrunchie. She pushed a stray hair out of her eyes and smiled weakly.

"I'm surprised you girls are still here," Ramona said.

Sophie stood at the bottom of the stairs, holding up the jump drive key ring. "I couldn't find my house key. I dropped it in the store."

"I'm glad you found it." Ramona was talking, but she wasn't really looking at the girls. She put her purse on the counter and sighed.

"Miss Brocklehurst? Ramona? How is Stanley?" Esther asked.

Ramona crossed the room in the dark to the fireplace, turned it on, and plopped down into the nearby wingback chair. The girls followed her. Esther sat in the opposite chair, and Sophie sat on a footstool.

"Well." She rubbed her eyes. "The doctor says that he is going to be fine. He has some head trauma, but with time and occupational therapy, that should heal. The biggest problem is a broken leg, and a fractured arm. They are both very painful."

"We are so sorry. Is there anything we can do to help?" Esther asked.

She smiled up at Esther, but her eyes drooped in exhaustion. "That's so sweet. I can't think of anything right now. Ash can help us with anything that requires lifting, and I can paint and fix just about anything. We just miss him, you know? He needs looking after, so we feel more like his moms than sisters, even if he is older."

"He's lucky to have you," Sophie said.

Esther put her shaking hands into her coat pockets. "When we were in the rare books room, I noticed he was selling some ink and books online. Do you need anyone to help? I know customers get upset when they've purchased something, and it doesn't arrive on time. I'd hate for him to lose a sale."

"Stanley? Selling things?" Ramona laughed softly.

Esther nodded. "I'm sure he was listing some ink, maybe? I watched over his shoulder."

Ramona rubbed her eyes. "Sometimes, I ask him to search our favorite website for a book or ink. But I'd never give him anything too important. He does get excited when older volumes come in. He has a good time looking them up on Google or eBay. I take him on buying trips sometimes or to garage sales to hunt for rare finds. He has a strange knack for finding valuable books in thrift stores or at yard sales." She smiled as if she had just shared a happy memory.

"Is there a reason he doesn't sell the books he finds?" Esther asked.

"He's dyslexic. It's one thing to find a book, it's another to list one and track sales. He may not be great at math or keeping track of sales, but he is an absolute mechanical genius. And he can build anything with just a photo of what I want. He also hand-painted the beautiful wooden sign outside the shop."

"He must be really talented at anything that he can do with his hands," Esther said.

"Anything but writing. His handwriting is atrocious, and his spelling is worse."

"Is he able to read?" Sophie asked.

"Oh, yes. He is a huge Tolkien fan. He is always searching for that special signed copy he believes he can find."

"We should let you rest. Is it possible to visit Stanley at the hospital?" Esther asked.

"What would you want to go up to that nasty place for?" Ramona asked.

"Because everyone should have their cast signed and a stash of chocolates in their hospital room," Sophie said.

Ramona laughed her musical laugh. "I quite agree."

Esther was just about to get into her Jeep when Alvah's car started. Alvah backed up and sped out of the parking lot.

The girls looked at each other and, without a word, jumped in the Jeep and followed her.

She drove toward Esther's house. Esther slowed so Alvah wouldn't see her Jeep when Alvah turned off the main highway, crossed the bridge, and parked in the trees in the parking lot by the ocean, just one block away from the Jameses' family home.

Esther rolled into the parking lot using the other entrance, with her headlights off. Alvah was just climbing out of her car and talking on her phone. She didn't seem to notice Esther, or the homeless man searching through the garbage on the Prom for cans.

The dog with the Santa hat barked once at Alvah before his owner yanked on his collar and shushed him.

Alvah passed their car without looking at it.

"What is she doing?" Sophie asked.

"Let's follow her."

Alvah ended her call just before she took the path to Ash's front door. The girls hid behind one of the tall trees that surrounded his little shingled cottage. The light was on inside, and Ash was making a video call at his desk. The screen was turned so they could see the video.

"Who is he talking to?" Esther asked.

Sophie adjusted her glasses, squinting. "It's too far away. I can't tell. Darn these eyes."

Alvah rapped on the door. They could hear Cookie bark and Ash telling her to be quiet. He closed his laptop, scooped up Cookie, and opened the door. The light from inside spilled out onto Alvah.

"I wish I could hear what she is saying," Esther said.

"Let's get closer," Sophie said.

The girls quickly moved and stood behind a tree closer to the house.

"I still can't hear anything." Esther pulled Sophie back into the shadows just as Ash stepped out of the door and Alvah reeled back.

"Don't ever come here again. I don't want to be seen with you!" Ash barked.

"You'll regret this," Alvah said.

"Don't threaten me." He went back inside and slammed the door.

Esther couldn't see Alvah's face in the dark, but her walk was definitely an angry march. She headed back to her car.

Esther motioned to Sophie to continue to follow Alvah. They hung back a little, giving her time to get to her car and start it.

When they reached the parking lot, Esther and Sophie stood in the trees by Alvah's car. She wasn't in it.

"Where is she?" Sophie hissed.

Santa, the dog, barked again.

"Hush, Killer," the can collector said. The girls moved through the trees toward the Promenade that ran the length of the ocean, and the man and dog.

The man was standing next to another garbage can, holding his dog by the collar, while the dog tugged and pulled his arm. Alvah handed him money. He closed the garbage can, loaded his collection, put the dog on a leash, and headed to the beach access, a cement slope that led to the sandy shore.

Alvah followed him. The girls followed Alvah.

The wind was blowing lightly on the beach, and the winter air was moist and foggy. The man's wagon had over inflated beach tires, perfect for pulling it through the grassy dunes. He headed north, over a dune, around a dune, past Sophie's house, which was lit up. They could see her parents at the table eating dinner. The man led Alvah past two empty vacation rentals and turned into the twisted Pacific pines that grew at the mouth of the Necanicum River, which poured into the sea.

Esther, Nephi, and Sophie had always called this tiny forest of trees "the end of the world." When they were in elementary school, and several times when Esther was in junior high, they built elaborate forts hidden in the trees. They spent hours trying to build a treehouse that always blew down with the next wind.

The fog closed in, and Esther stopped. Sophie tapped her arm and pointed. The red Santa hat had gone to the south a little and down a trail.

The girls stayed behind trees and ferns until the wagon pulled into a clearing with a small fire. Several men and women sat around the fire. One woman was nursing a baby. A girl that Esther had seen on the school bus with Mary was sleeping in a man's lap. Esther supposed that was her father.

There were four or five tents and lean-tos hidden in the trees, with a pile of garbage next to them.

"I can't believe we didn't know this was here," Sophie said.

Esther leaned close to Sophie so she could whisper. "I can. Mom and Papa J were talking about places like this the other day. He said twenty-five kids are on record at the high school as not having a permanent address. He was forced to toss families out of tents they had pitched on private property in view of the mayor's home. He said there were kids living there."

"Can't somebody do something?" Sophie asked.

"That's what he and Mom were talking about. Mom has some ideas. But everything costs money."

Alvah came out of one of the tents with the can collector following her. And then Kol came out of the same tent.

* * *

Esther drove home from the parking lot. They pulled up in front of the James house, and she shut the Cherokee off. Both girls fell back in their seats and sighed.

"It's like a Charles Dickens nightmare," Esther said.

"I almost died when I saw that baby," Sophie said.

Esther's stomach was in knots. "I thought my heart was going to stop."

"I had no idea..."

"I want to take back every mean thing I ever said about Kol. No wonder he's always angry. How does he stay so clean?"

"That's why he always wears black. Same jeans, same T-shirt, same coat, and they don't show dirt." Sophie shrugged.

"Oh, biscuits."

"Jinx," they both said and started to giggle nervously. It was the kind of laughter she made when she was so tired, and had cried so hard, she was slaphappy.

When the laughing subsided, Esther took her keys out of the ignition but didn't make a move to get out of the car.

"I am still trying to figure out what Alvah was doing there," Esther said.

"Or why she gave him money and followed him back to his camp. He must know her from somewhere," Sophie said.

"Maybe from Kol?" Esther chewed on her lower lip, trying to think. "I am too tired to make sense of it all. All I can think about is those poor kids."

Sophie checked her phone. "It's only seven o'clock, and yet it feels like it's midnight. What do you want to do?"

"You should go home and get some rest," Esther said.

"Rest? Have you ever known me to rest?"

Esther chuckled. "Only when your batteries run out and you wind down like the Energizer Bunny."

"The who?"

"You'd have to watch *Murder She Wrote* reruns with Grandma Mable. The commercials are even reruns. You know, made for old people."

"Isn't she like, sixty?"

Esther nodded.

"I hope she doesn't die soon," Sophie said. "She should live to be ninety. What would we do without her?"

"That's a question I never want to have to answer."

"Do you want to come over?"

"Actually, I have a little Christmas project I have to finish by tomorrow," Esther said.

"Oh! A gift for me?"

Esther shook her head no but couldn't help giggling.

"Well, if it's for Parker, and it's mushy, you can do it alone," Sophie said.

"It's a surprise," Esther said.

"Fine. But it would be better if you had my expertise." Sophie got out of the Jeep. "See you in the a.m." She closed the door and walked toward her home, a few houses down on the ocean side of the street.

Esther didn't like the thought of spending the evening without Sophie and would have loved her help, but this was something she needed to do alone. She hated crying in front of people.

18

—•—

E sther lifted herself into the dusty attic and turned on her cell phone flashlight. She stood and realized the attic was much smaller than she remembered, or she was taller. She hadn't been in the attic for years. It was Nephi's job to haul big things up and down the ladder.

It took her several minutes to move boxes and reach the brown chest she wanted. It was also smaller than she remembered.

She was eight when she took the pictures off her walls in her bedroom and packed them into this box. It had been sealed since that day. Tears were already pooling in her eyes, and she hadn't even opened the box. She dragged it across the attic floor as quietly as she could. She didn't want her mother to know what she was doing, and she definitely didn't want Mary to find out.

Before she took it down the ladder, she poked her head out of the small opening and checked the landing seventeen feet below. *It's a good thing I'm not afraid of heights.*

Slowly, she slid the trunk out of the opening while hanging onto its leather handle on the side. Lying on her belly, she searched for the top rung of the ladder with her feet. Once she got her footing, she climbed down the ladder using one hand while clinging onto the leather handle on the side of the trunk as it swung free. She felt as if the arm carrying the weight of the trunk was going to pop out of its socket. Finally, she reached the floor.

She quickly took the trunk to her room before she returned, took down the ladder, and put it back in the closet it came from.

She looked around, amazed that no one had heard the noise of the ladder, or if they had, no one had come upstairs. Once she was inside her room, she shut and locked the door.

Her hands shook as she opened the lid. She smiled and wept when she saw Stinky Bear, pink and bedraggled, on top of the pile of papers inside. She picked her up and smelled her. Underneath the musty odor, she still smelled of the cloves Grandma Mable had sewn inside before she sewed a smile under her black button eyes.

She loved Stinky Bear, but just like everything else, she had wanted to forget Stinky Bear. The last time she'd held the bear she was hiding from her father and her mother was bleeding while sirens came closer and closer.

Tonight, she didn't want to put her down. She had been a faithful friend. For some reason, she felt ready to remember all the nights Stinky Bear had kept her company, and her grandma's hands as she sewed on Stinky Bear's eyes.

Her kindergarten report card was under the bear. She smiled when she saw her teacher's name, Miss Jackson, and remembered how she had held Esther when she skinned her knees and ruined her tights on the playground. She opened the report card. Perfect grades. All the years of trying to be perfect while perfection never saved her... she laughed at herself.

Miss Molly meowed at the door, and Esther let her in. "Perfection isn't magic, Miss Molly. It isn't armor. You are magic, Grandma Mable is magic, and so are all my friends."

Under the report card, there was a shoebox. It held what she needed. She went to her desk and got out the eleven-by-eighteen-inch parchment paper she asked Grandma Mable to buy for her. She had three glue sticks, one pink stapler, and pink scissors. She spread them out on the floor along with her calligraphy set.

A few hours later, she dropped a pen and realized she was falling asleep while writing. It was time to call it a day. She had one more thing to do. She signed her handwritten note and pasted it into her project. She put her gift in a Christmas box and wrapped it. Using a sharpie, she addressed it.

Miss Molly woke Esther. She had stayed up too late. Her head was pounding. After she ran to the bathroom, she opened the chest and put her supplies in it. She moved the chest to the foot of her bed and covered it with the afghan Grandma Mable had crocheted for her when she was ten.

After she was dressed for school, she quietly made her way downstairs with the package, through the kitchen and through the door that led to Grandma Mable's apartment. A short flight of stairs took her down to the lower level.

Grandma Mable's pale blue sitting room was made for reading and movie nights. She had a faux electric fireplace surrounded by an overstuffed chintzy couch and chairs. Her television hung over the mantle, scrolling through family photos. The lights were off, except for a small lamp.

She could hear Nephi singing in the shower down the hall. Esther quietly knocked on her grandmother's bedroom door. A light came on, shining under the door.

"Come in," Grandma Mable said.

Esther peeked in. Grandma Mable's reading lamp was on. She was wearing a flannel nighty, rubbing her eyes, and stretching.

"Hi, sweetie. What can I do for you?"

"Are you busy today?" Esther asked.

"I promised to work for Ash this afternoon at Literal Buns so he could get some personal things done. Other than that, I'm all yours."

"Would you consider mailing a package for me? It needs to be sent using overnight mail, or as fast as it can go."

"I hate to say it but there is no overnight air in Necanicum," Grandma Mable said. "Everything goes to Portland first. If I get it to the post office right when they open, Franny might help me get it on the morning truck."

"I'm so sorry I didn't get it done and mailed sooner. I know it'll be expensive. I'll pay you back. We got our first paycheck."

"Pay me back after Christmas. I'm sure you have some friends to buy gifts for." Grandma Mable took the package, paused, and ran her hand over the name and address. "When do you talk to him next?"

"We have a video call with his therapist early Christmas Eve." Esther sat on the end of the bed.

"What do you call him now?"

"Dad. He may be just my bio-dad, but not every moment with him was a bad one. And Parker once told me, love doesn't run out. The more you have, the more you have and the more you give, the more you have... or something like that." She smiled.

"You should embroider that on a throw pillow." Mable chuckled. She opened her arms and gave Esther a hug.

"What's he singing?"

"'Sgt. Pepper's Lonely Hearts Club Band.' You know, the Beatles. My favorite." She got out of her bed and followed Esther down the hall.

Grandma Mable knocked on the bathroom door. "Listen, Ringo, your mom needs the bathroom. Hurry it up!"

Laughing, Esther followed the smell of bacon back up the stairs to find Papa J and Sophie eating breakfast.

"Where's Mary?" Esther asked.

Papa J took a drink of his orange juice, wiped his mouth, and said, "She's still asleep, and your mom's already out on a call."

"Good. More bacon for me," Esther said.

"Hey now!" Sophie grabbed three pieces off the serving platter and added them to the two she had.

Esther made herself a bowl of oatmeal and brown sugar, and sat across the table from Papa J and Sophie. It wasn't long before Nephi came into the kitchen in jeans and a clean white T-shirt, and grabbed bacon off Sophie's plate. She tried to stab his hand with her fork.

Esther looked at Papa J, who was busy scrolling through his phone. "Papa J?"

He looked up.

"Raini didn't do anything wrong. Ash Corradao had the exact same inkwell in his house," Esther said.

"Leave Ash out of this. He's a standup guy," Nephi said.

Papa J leaned back, looked at Nephi, and squinted at her. "How would you know what Ash has?"

"When we walked the other night, the lights were on inside his house. He didn't have the curtains closed. I just happened to notice. It was in plain sight."

"You didn't go into his house?" Papa J asked.

"His windows are very clean," Sophie said.

Papa J closed his eyes and looked as if he was trying not to laugh. "I see. Well, just so that you know, the chief has taken over the case because of the community and the mayor's concern, and the fact that the accident made Portland News. He says he has more reason to arrest you than any person on his suspect list. He also thinks I should ground you until you agree to move to another country."

"Rude!" Sophie exclaimed.

"He also had a chat with your father, Sophie. He can't believe that your father believes every word that comes out of your, and I quote the chief, 'lying little mouth,' with the emphasis on little."

"Holy guacamole, he's seriously rude!" Sophie folded her arms.

"I assured him that I would make both of you pay for your crimes by doing household chores like cleaning toilets. That seemed to placate him. So now I have to be a man of my word."

"We've got to go to school." Sophie left her plate on the table and ran for the door.

Esther stayed behind. "I saw the camp."

Papa J tipped his head. "The camp?"

"The homeless camp the kids live in."

"The one by the old mill pond? Or the one by Shaver park?"

"A different one."

"Another one?" Papa J asked.

Esther nodded.

"Where is it?"

She looked at his face.

He leaned toward her across the table, earnest eyes drawn together in concern.

"I am not telling you."

Deflated, he fell back into his chair. "Why?"

"Because then you have to do something about it."

After Esther left the house, she stopped on the porch, sat on the swing next to Sophie, and created a new group text. She included Sophie, Grandma Mable, Nephi, Parker, Paisley, and Bridget. She named the group, the Bacon Gang.

Text to Bacon Gang: *Can we meet tonight at Literal Buns after we close the store?*

Text from Paisley to Bacon Gang: *What's on the agenda?*

Text from Esther to Bacon Gang: *Murder.*

Text from Sophie to Bacon Gang: *I'm in.*

Esther laughed. "I'm sitting right here."

"Get with the Gen Z way, E."

19

— • —

Nephi and Parker opened the back of the medical supply van and helped Wilber Dunlevy unload a hospital bed and some type of other pole or equipment. They rolled, lifted, turned, and dragged it into the spacious kitchen at the back of the store.

After they moved the table out of the breakfast nook, they set the bed up. Ramona told them where to mount a television on the wall so it could be seen from the bed. She put a Lord of the Rings garbage can next to it, with a cell phone and charger.

Wilbur brought in a rolling table that would slide over the bed so Stanley would have a place to put his water and meals.

Esther and Sophie watched in between customers. Esther found a small ceramic Christmas tree that was on the mantle, brought it in, and put it on his table.

"I have an idea." Sophie rummaged in the hall closet and came out with a box of twinkle lights they hadn't used on the tree. Using masking tape, Esther and Sophie taped the lights around all the windows in the breakfast nook and moved one of the wreaths from the store window into the window over the bed.

When they were finished, they all stood back and admired their work.

"I hear a truck," Ramona said. "I bet it's the ambulance. Thanks, Nephi, Parker. I will pay you. And Wilbur, send us the bill."

"We won't take your money," Nephi said. Parker nodded.

Ramona smiled. "You kids are something wonderful. Let's bring him home, shall we?"

They followed her to the porch and watched the medical transport ambulance drivers unload Stanley, with Desdemona at his side. Stanley gave them a Stanley sort of sideways smile and waved.

"Welcome home!" Ramona called and held her arms out, walking to the gurney and hugging her big brother.

In his slow drawl, Stanley said, "It's good to be home."

Desdemona carried large plastic bags marked with the hospital logo from the van to the porch and went back for a box of medicine.

"Here. Let us help you," Esther said.

"Thank you, girls," Desdemona said.

A small, older woman in the store stopped perusing books and looked over her cat-eye glasses. "I heard someone was injured in an accident. Are you okay?"

"I'm home." Stanley was still smiling and waving.

Once Stanley was off the gurney, tucked into his bed, and the ambulance pulled away, he yawned.

"Is Alvah here?" Stanley asked.

"I'm sure she'll be over later. Can we get you anything?" Ramona asked him while holding his hand.

"A remote control and a bowl of ice cream. The Andy Griffith Show has reruns on Prime, and I'm only on the fifth season."

Stanley's right leg was in a cast, resting on a pillow. His right arm was also in a full cast and propped up with pillows. He was still smiling as he yawned.

Mrs. Winters, a teacher in Esther's school, came in with another woman Esther didn't recognize. They seemed to be arguing.

Mrs. Winters pulled a book off the shelf in the mystery section. "I'm telling you this is the perfect book for the mystery book club. You and I are more than halfway through, and we still can't agree on who the killer is."

The other woman shook her head. "I always guess the end. I am telling you the priest is the killer." They both kept looking through the shelves.

"You're wrong. How could he be? He's too nice? And what is his motive?" Mrs. Winters asked.

"Love and money. What else?" the other woman said.

"I have such a hard time suspecting a priest. I know they make mistakes, but he is just so nice."

Esther's mind began to spin. Something about their conversation took her back. Her father was standing at the barbecue arguing with Mr. Johnson, the neighbor. She could still see it.

Mr. Johnson said, "He's innocent, I tell you. He is really a nice guy. Someone set him up. I knew him!"

Her father emphasized his point by waving the tongs, which made Esther worry that he would hit Mr. Johnson as he had hit her mother. She remembered holding her breath and wishing the argument would stop.

"All I know is he is serving a lengthy sentence in prison. If a jury of his peers thinks he's guilty, then he is," her father said.

The only other thing she could remember from that day was jumping on the Johnson's trampoline while the Johnson boys and another kid from the block had the same argument their parents had. She remembered wondering why it mattered so much.

"Remember, the priest injured his hand. I think the bandage is covering a burn," Mrs. Winters's friend said.

Mrs. Johnson shook her head and put the book on the counter in front of Esther.

"Can you order more copies of this book? I want to send mystery book club members in to buy them over the next month," Mrs. Winters said.

Esther was lost in thought.

"Esther?"

"Ah, yes. I think. Can we, Sophie? I will have to ask Ramona, I mean the store owner," Esther stammered.

"I'll wait."

"She isn't here."

Sophie stepped in front of her. "Give me your phone number. I will check and get back to you. In the meantime, let me write down the book's title, author, and ISBN number."

Then it struck Esther. She remembered the crime her father and friend were arguing about. Esther loved reading the comics in the newspaper and, already at a young age, paid attention to the news. They had sparked her curiosity. She had asked Grandma Mable at the time, who told her the story. Thoughts and puzzle pieces were coming together so fast she was afraid they would fly away before she could catch them all.

Esther pulled out her cell phone. "I have to take a break."

Sophie nodded in acknowledgment, and Esther walked to the kitchen while searching for the crime.

Esther opened the door to the Literal Buns café and was immediately immersed in the smell of banana nut bread.

"My stomach is growling. Are we going to eat while we sleuth?" Sophie asked.

Smiling, Esther put her things in a chair in the only booth in the bakery. "Did you know the brain consumes about twenty percent of the body's energy, which translates to an average of about three hundred calories daily? Of course, we're going to eat. Let's hurry up and buy something before they close."

"My brain burns triple that amount. It's no wonder I am always hungry," Sophie said.

"Hi, girls," Grandma Mable called from the kitchen. "I sent Bubba home so I could try my hand at banana nut bread."

"I didn't know you knew how to bake," Esther said.

Grandma Mable hung her apron up. "How hard can it be? You just follow a recipe."

Esther pushed another table over and made sure there were enough chairs.

"Does Ash have his own recipes? I want his cinnamon roll recipe," Sophie said.

"I googled banana nut bread," Grandma Mable said. "I watched a YouTube tutorial. The girl on the video talked fast, so I hope it turns out."

Christmas music played softly in the background. Grandma Mable used a paper plate to collect a variety of baked goods from the glass case.

Nephi and Parker came out of the kitchen to join them. Parker gave her a sweet kiss on her cheek and sat next to her, with his arm over the back of her chair.

"The dishes are done, and Parker mopped the floor and wiped down the appliances," Nephi said.

"Here's Paisley," Parker said. He nodded toward his father's old BMW sedan as it pulled into the parking lot.

"Oh good. Madison and Bridget are with her," Esther said.

Nephi rolled his eyes. "We're outnumbered again, bro."

Parker laughed.

Madison Merriweather and her daughter had once been suspects when Parker's sister, Paisley, and his mother, Melissa, disappeared. It wasn't until Madison's bestselling book was made into a movie and Esther and Sophie traveled to her stone castle built on the Northern Washington Coast that they finally got to know Madison and Bridget.

Every one of Madison's books were bestsellers, and now one was a movie. Bridget was almost as talented as her mother. Even though she hadn't officially recorded her songs, she was gaining a reputation at school as a singer and songwriter.

"Okay, people. Who is going to take notes and who is in charge of the meeting?" Paisley was known for her organizational skills. Paisley was as practical and as organized as her best friend, Bridget, was creative and artistic.

"Are you volunteering?" Grandma Mable wiggled her brows and smiled.

"Of course." Paisley opened her bag and pulled out a legal pad and a clear pencil box with a rainbow of markers, pens, pencils, and highlighters.

"Where do we start?" Bridget asked.

Before she could answer, the bakery door opened, and Kol came in. Surprised to see the group, he turned around and tried to get back out the door unnoticed.

"Kol, buddy. What do you need?" Nephi asked.

Kol frowned. "I was looking for Ash or Alvah." He went out the door and let it slam shut. Nephi got up and locked the door, turned the open sign to closed, and turned off the porch light.

"I wonder what he wants with Ash and Alvah," Sophie whispered to Esther.

"Does anyone want tea? I can make a pot?" Madison volunteered.

"No need. I will bring out some sodas and put it on my tab." Mable wasn't gone long before she returned with a variety of canned soda pop and a loaf of banana nut bread on a small breadboard.

"Shall we get started?" Paisley asked.

"Sophie and I have some information to add to our last conversation," Esther said.

"I will put Hazel and Stanley at the top of the page as our prime victims even though Stanley lived," Paisley said.

Esther nodded in agreement. "Exactly. What do Hazel and Stanley have in common?" She looked around the table and waited. Madison shook her head, and Nephi shrugged.

Esther opened her phone and showed them a screenshot of the Egyptian inkwell she found on Google. Esther put her phone down and began.

"Before the banister broke and Hazel fell, she had found some ink and quills that excited her. We now know what else was in that box."

Paisley wrote the word *box* and waited to list the contents.

"Ramona bought the box from the store when it closed," Esther continued. "She found an inkwell like this one and some ink she thought might be from the 1800s, if the labels on the bottles are correct. The ink bottle was still sealed. Stanley was researching ink, inkwells, and books online before he had his accident. Sophie and I located an online account in Stanley's name on a well-known auction site for rare books, ink, inkwells, and other items related to books and reading. Ash has a similar inkwell in his house..."

"Nephi and I think it isn't Ash. After working with him, we don't think he could have done it," Parker said.

"Seriously? Haven't we always said sometimes killers are your nice next-door neighbor," Sophie said. "Haven't you heard reporters interview serial killers' neighbors? They always say what a nice guy the killer was."

Grandma Mable chuckled.

Esther held her hand up as if she were in school to get everyone's attention. "Hang on. There's more. A similar inkwell was planted in Raini's locker to get her in trouble or point the finger at her."

"Like the book and bolts were planted in your car," Grandma Mable said.

"Exactly. So the inkwell, ink, quills, and possibly rare books are what the murder of Hazel and the attempted murder of Stanley have in common." Esther looked around the table.

Madison Merriweather leaned forward. "Go on."

"The other thing both murders have in common is Alvah." Esther sat back and let that sink in.

"But she wasn't there when the shelves fell on Stanley," Nephi said.

"The bolts could have been removed at any time. Just because she and Draven gave each other an alibi doesn't mean she isn't involved. And her name is on the auction account with Stanley. The money they spent and received came from her account and went back to her account. Interestingly, Ramona says Stanley is not capable of running an account or book sales because he is dyslexic and has serious challenges when it comes to math, accounts, and managing something like an auction."

Madison stood. Her mouth fell open. She looked around the room and sat down hard. "There it is! It must be Alvah. Esther James and Sophie Ito, you're brilliant."

Esther shook her head. "Wait, we aren't sure it's Alvah yet. Let me give you the rest of the pieces we know so far. There are still a lot of questions to be answered. But I have something that ties it all together, I hope. Something about the ink and this whole thing had me thinking. Coincidentally, it isn't the first time I have heard about old ink used in a crime. Sophie helped me sort out the uses for ink online.

Sophie grinned and wiggled her brows. "She couldn't have done it without me."

"What do you mean coincidentally? And how do I write this all down?" Paisley asked.

Sophie pointed at the page. "List the items that become the motive, like the inkwell and the online account. Write the names of everyone involved with each item."

"Thank heavens I chose to use a pencil. Keep going," Paisley said. Head down, she cleaned up her paper.

"I know it's confusing, but when I tell you the coincidence, I think it will all come together. There are very few missing pieces now," Esther said.

"What's the motive?" Grandma Mable asked.

Sophie pointed at the ink on the paper. "The ink, inkwells, and books. They can be extremely valuable depending on dates, editions, signatures, and rarity. We could see that Stanley and Alvah have currently listed over one hundred thousand dollars of items on their joint account."

"What is the coincidence?" Parker asked.

"I remembered something from when I was a child and we lived in Salt Lake City. We had a neighbor who went to jail before I was born, but my dad's friend knew him. Even though he had been found guilty of killing several people, dad's friend was arguing that he was innocent. The argument happened during a backyard barbecue. All of this brought back the memory."

"I kept having bad dreams, and then it finally came together. Today, I googled the nature of the crime and the city it occurred in and found this article." Esther held up her phone so they could see the news headline.

"Forgery and Murder" was the title. The tagline read, "Serial killer used stolen paper and antique ink to forge documents worth over a million dollars."

"Look at the date. That's when a million dollars meant something," Sophie said.

Madison and Grandma Mable laughed.

"It's still a lot of money if you haven't sold thirty million books and the movie rights," Madison said, tipping her head and winking at Grandma Mable.

"Wait. What kinds of documents and how did he do it?" Paisley asked.

All eyes were on Esther, who thought about how to put so much information into a few short sentences.

Esther chewed her fingernail. Grandma Mable pulled Esther's arm down.

"Sorry. It's like this. He went into the university library and a museum and used a razor blade to cut blank back pages out of rare and ancient books. He used the appropriately aged ink to create documents that would be worth money, like a personal note from someone like Benjamin Franklin that would be controversial," Esther said.

"Why would it be controversial?" Parker asked.

"Good question. Sometimes his documents showed that famous people had affairs or did things that would cast them in a bad light. People who loved Benjamin Franklin or whoever the documents were about, would buy them to destroy them. People who hated the person the documents were about would pay to have them to destroy the famous person's reputation."

Esther continued. "It's really genius if you think about it. Both parties would get into a bidding war and both parties would want the sale kept secret to control the information in the document. I guess he got away with it for years. But when he thought someone was onto his scam, he killed them, and then the next person, and the next person who found out what he was doing.

"I'm kind of oversimplifying the story, but it got me thinking. The ink Hazel found is in jars that are dated. It could be used to forge signatures in first editions to increase their value. It could also be used to write a personal letter from someone like Agatha Christie, explaining where she went when she disappeared."

Esther took a deep breath. "The beauty of it is, if you tried to carbon date it or checked the paper for authenticity, it would check out. The paper would be from the time of her disappearance if the killer found a book published that year. The ink would also be from that year or the previous year. See? Genius really."

Madison fell back in her seat. "Well, I'm stunned. I think you've just given me the plot for my next novel. That's cunning and evil. But why kill people?"

Sophie adjusted her glasses. "To avoid getting caught and to continue to make large amounts of money."

Nephi shook his head. "Maybe so, but you already said Stanley isn't that smart. Alvah didn't even know Stanley when Hazel was killed."

Esther looked at the names Paisley had written on the paper and was now erasing and moving around the page. She chewed on her bottom lip and glanced at Sophie.

"Maybe someone was helping them. We followed Alvah after we found her name on the account. She went to Ash's, and they had an argument. Maybe they were working together and had a falling out. Then she paid a man who lives in a homeless camp a wad of cash. Kol was also there and talked to her. Kol could have removed the bolts while he was working."

Nephi stood. "I keep telling you I'm sure it isn't Ash."

"How do you know?" Parker asked him.

"I just have a feeling about him. He doesn't seem sinister or that evil."

"He did go to prison for something he did as a stupid kid. He's paid his price," Grandma Mable said.

Nephi folded his arms and sat down. "You haven't mentioned Kol or Ramona's stupid boyfriend, Raven." He cut two pieces of banana bread and gave one to Paisley, who didn't seem to notice.

"Draven." Sophie corrected him.

"He's definitely not very nice. He was more worried about his books than he was about poor Stanley," Parker said.

Nephi took a bite of banana nut bread, scrunched his face up, took a napkin, and spit it out.

"We still don't have all the pieces," Esther said.

The bakery door opened, making the bells on the door tinkle. Parker's grandfather came in, beaming.

"Are you ready to go, Mable?" Lord Stuart asked.

"In a minute, James. Come on in," Grandma Mable said.

Parker looked wide eyed at Esther and mouthed, "James?"

Esther, suppressing a laugh, shook her head and shrugged. She whispered. "I'm clueless."

"Alright, Esther. Let's wrap this up and figure out what we need to do," Grandma Mable said.

"Next steps," Paisley said out loud, but more to herself as she neatly wrote the words.

"I think you take what you know to your father, Papa J," Madison Merriweather said.

"I agree," Bridget said. Paisley and Parker echoed her.

"What do you think?" Esther looked directly at Nephi.

"I think we use you for bait and when you're eaten like a worm on the hook, we'll know who the killer is," Nephi said. He gave her a cheesy grin. Sophie buddy-punched him with her tiny fist.

"Madison. Would you like to join us?" Lord Stuart asked.

"I don't want to get in the way," Madison said.

"Nonsense. We'll grab Marion and make it a foursome. I'll bring my banana nut bread," Grandma Mable said.

Nephi's brows raised, and he looked at Esther. "I could get you some day-old cinnamon rolls instead of the bread."

"Nonsense. The bread's fine." Grandma Mable took it over to the counter to put it in a bag.

Madison brightened up. "Bridget? Can you go home with Paisley?"

"Seriously, Mom?"

"It'll be fun," Paisley said.

Sophie leaned close to Esther's ear. "Is your grandmother dating Parker's grandfather?"

Esther looked at Sophie and crossed her eyes and suppressed a giggle.

"Holy guacamole."

"Wait! Before we all go our separate ways, I have another item to bring to the committee's attention," Paisley said. Parker chuckled and grinned at his twin.

Paisley paused, looking around the table, waiting for everyone to be quiet. "Bridget and I have been talking. We heard Raini's mom has cancer. Bridget said in America people sub for Santa and secretly give gifts to families who need help. I vote we all sub for Santa for Raini."

"We become the substitute Santas for Raini," Bridget said.

"Can we put it to a vote? Do we have your support? We would all have to chip in," Paisley said.

"I will donate five hundred pounds," Lord Stuart said.

"Now you're impressing me, James." Grandma Mable got up and patted him on the shoulder.

"All in favor say aye, all opposed say nay," Paisley said.

Everyone said aye.

"Then it's decided," Paisley said. "Christmas break begins at noon on Thursday. We will get out of classes early. Bridget and I will shop for the family. Grandma Mable, can you use your stealth to find out what they need?"

"I will call the school counselor and see if she has been over and knows," Grandma Mable said.

"I want to pitch in too," Madison said.

"Mom. You can't pay for everything. We can do this," Bridget said.

Madison frowned for only a second. "Alright, darling. Do let me know if you need my money."

"I want to add one more name to our list of people we help this Christmas," Esther said.

The group quieted, and when she had their attention, she said, "Kol."

20

E sther hugged Parker goodbye and started the Jeep for the short drive home from Literal Buns. Sophie was silent until the parking lot was empty.

"Aren't we leaving?" Sophie asked.

"In a minute. I can't forget how Draven used Alvah for an alibi, and my suspicion is that they are working together, or at the very least, cheating on Ramona."

"I know. I love Ramona. She told me he went to Portland today or something. You know, buying books. He sure wasn't around to help us get Stanley set up." Sophie took her glasses off and cleaned them with a cloth from her backpack.

"At first, I wasn't sure about Ramona, but she reminds me of Ms. Priest. When I saw how much she loved Stanley, I couldn't imagine her planning a murder for money."

"We need to know more about Alvah, don't we?" Sophie said.

"Yup. Do you want to go on another nighttime walk?"

Sophie sighed. "Sure."

"Let's move the Jeep out of the parking lot and circle around to her tiny house." Esther started the car and rolled it out of sight a block away from the store.

The air was crisp, but not as cold as the last time they staked out Alvah's house. Once again, they stayed in the trees.

The lights were on in the living room, letting Esther and Sophie watch what was going on like a television show. Alvah and Draven were sitting next to each other on the couch, having heated words. Once again, Esther could only hear every other word, but there was no doubt about the anger written all over their faces or the tone of the disagreement. "Whatever it is, it's serious. And he definitely isn't out of town," Sophie said.

"One thing is for sure. We know that he has been lying to Ramona. That looks more like a lovers quarrel than a debate between friends or acquaintances. She is red in the face. See how she is leaning toward him and the small amount of space between them?"

"Cheese and crackers, they're close, aren't they? Let's get out of here."

"We need to figure out how they're linked," Esther said. "There must be something online."

Since it was technically a school night, Esther dropped Sophie off at home.

"Text me, okay?" Sophie asked.

"You text me. I'm going to research Alvah. Can you research Draven Kane?"

"I will have something in less than an hour," Sophie promised.

"I'm going to beat you by ten minutes," Esther said.

"Game on."

Miss Molly was waiting at the door for Esther, or so she liked to believe. The truth was, her food bowl was empty, and she was meowing at Esther angrily while they walked to the kitchen to her bowl.

"Sorry, Miss Molly. Today was a little long. I'm surprised Mary didn't feed you." Esther opened a small can of cat food and spooned it into Miss Molly's bowl.

It only took a few minutes for Miss Molly to lick her bowl clean and hop onto Esther's lap. She picked up her beloved cat and looked up the three flights of stairs to get to her room.

"They seem longer tonight," Esther said, carrying Miss Molly and still wearing her laptop in a backpack, with other info from the library.

When Esther made it to the top floor, she passed her mother's bedroom door.

"Is that you, Esther?" Her mother called from inside her room.

"Yes, Mom, it's me."

"You're late. I had Mary feed Miss Molly. I also put some clean laundry on the chest at the foot of your bed. Why do you have your chest?"

"I'm just making some Christmas presents this year and wanted to copy some of the old photos in the box."

"Sounds good. Good night, honey."

Esther looked down at Miss Molly, who looked up at her. "Don't look at me like that. You're not innocent, you conniving kitty. You'll make yourself sick if you eat two meals a night."

Esther took Miss Molly into her room and put her in her adorable mint green cat basket, knowing she wouldn't stay there for a second. It had been a terrible waste of money.

As predicted, the cat leapt onto the bed and watched Esther slip on a long, white cotton nightgown. Esther turned off the overhead light and turned on the lamp on her bedside table.

She put her headphones on and turned on her favorite playlist, My Life is a Movie. She pulled her laptop onto the bed and began to google. Before a minute passed, her phone pinged.

Text from Sophie: *I win. Did you see it?*

Text from Esther: *No fair. I had to feed Miss Molly.*

Text from Sophie: *I thought Mary did that at night.*

Text from Esther: *We both fed her.*

Text from Sophie: *Yes, but did you read it? Here's the link.*

Esther opened the link. It was a newspaper article from The Washington Post. Draven Kane and Alvah Sable were in the photo, shaking hands with someone. The article read, "Smithsonian receives rare documents once belonging to JFK from Hubris House Rare Books and Document Dealers located in Maryland."

Text from Esther: *Holy guacamole! They're in it together, like we thought.*

Text from Sophie: *No need to food swear. LOL You're usually right.*

Text from Esther: *Now we need to figure out how they did it.*

Text from Sophie: *Time to bait a trap and prove it.*

Text from Esther: *TTYL Night*

Text from Sophie: *Night!*

21

— . —

E sther rolled over again. This time her blanket fell off the bed onto the floor. She squished her pillow and ignored the blanket. *Sleep, please come, please.* She rolled back the other way, and Miss Molly walked across the bed, kneaded her hair, made a nest, and snuggled in.

"That's one way of making me lie still."

Pictures, memories, all the pieces of the puzzles spun around in her mind like a mad carousel with Draven, Kol, Ash, and Alvah riding round and round. When she did drop off to sleep, she had dreams that ran into nightmares, where Alvah was chasing her with money and Kol was always lurking.

At four-thirty in the morning, the noise of the can collector on the street woke her up. She looked at the window.

"Well, Miss Molly, we might as well get up. Let's get to the bottom of this rat's nest."

Esther felt her curly long hair and pulled some around and looked at it.

"We'll take care of the rat's nest on my head later."

She brought her laptop to her bed and propped herself up on a pile of pillows. Miss Molly tried to walk across her keyboard.

After an hour of combing through social media, she still had nothing. She tried to find arrest records for Maryland, but their website only listed a phone number she would have to call to request records. If she wanted to access records, there would be a fee and she would have to make phone calls.

My dad has an inmate number. I wonder if I can find a prison record. She searched .gov prison inmate locator. The Federal Bureau of Prisons Find an Inmate search system was on the page beneath a list of ads offering criminal record searches for a fee.

The federal website allowed her to search by number or name. First, she put in *Alvah*. A record popped up with her name. It said the inmate was fifty-four. Esther didn't know Alvah's age, but thought she looked younger. It listed a release date, but it didn't have the prison name or location. She had been released ten years ago.

When she clicked on Alvah's name, it opened her inmate page and gave links for calling, emailing, sending packages, or sending money.

"I know how to find the location, Miss Molly."

She clicked on the link for shipping packages to inmates. A few clicks later and she had the prison mailing address and the state Alvah had been released from.

Next, she looked up Draven Kane. Nothing. Then she had an idea. She looked up just Draven. Nothing again. Then she searched for his last name. On the short list was someone named Raven. Raven was male and had been released in the same year Alvah had been. He had also served his sentence in the same federal prison.

"Yes!" She raised both her fists in triumph, waking Miss Molly.

"Sorry."

She texted the Bacon Gang. She shared what they had learned last night and this morning. The last line read, *Someone must talk to Ramona. I guess that's Soph and me.*

After she sent all the information, she realized it was only six in the morning.

Oops! I hope they had their phones silenced. She lay back down for just a minute and fell into a deep sleep until her alarm went off at seven.

22

Esther pulled the Jeep into the school parking lot. The girls hesitated to get out of the warm truck and walk in the winter fog to the library doors.

"Hey. I know sometimes you write to your bio-dad. Did you send him a card or anything? Because if you do, I want to help. I could bake a cake with a file in it." Sophie said.

Esther looked down and fidgeted with a loose string on the steering-wheel cover. "It doesn't matter. I might have blown it anyway by not sending it earlier. Grandma Mable mailed it for me. Hopefully it gets there before my call."

Sophie looked at her. "You amaze me, E. I know you've made peace with him, but I couldn't do what you're doing."

Esther adjusted her messy bun in the mirror and took a deep breath. "Honestly, I don't know what I'm doing. When he asked me to forgive him, it was the hardest thing I've ever done. But then I learned that forgiving him was more about me letting go. It felt great to release and not hold on to it like a black cloud following me everywhere."

"Yeah, but how do you trust him not to do it again?"

Esther looked down at the thread and tried unsuccessfully to tuck it under the steering-wheel cover. "I don't. I mean, I trust me."

"And me, I hope." Sophie smiled.

"Grandma Mable said something I really liked. I could speak to him or not. I get to choose whatever relationship I am comfortable with. At the same time, I can set my own boundaries and honor them. You know? It's like intentionally risking, because I trust myself to make good decisions and to honor my own boundaries."

Sophie's brows raised. "Holy blah blah. That's a mouthful. All I know is that if anyone tried to kidnap either of us, I would forgive them while I showed them my mad Jiu-Jitsu skills."

"It is a lot of blah blah, isn't it?" Esther laughed nervously. "The execution of it all is still a challenge. I've learned to trust the Bacon Gang and my family, but bringing someone else into my circle of trust is another matter. I still can't wrap my head around Nephi protecting Ash when we know he killed someone." She chewed her thumbnail.

Sophie touched Esther's hand. "Leave some fingernail behind."

Esther chuckled. "Okay, Mom!"

They got out of the Jeep and put their backpacks on.

"Crepes. We dressed alike again. We're like an old couple in matching jogging suits."

Esther looked down at her fisherman's sweater, jeans, and Hunter boots. Then she looked at Sophie and chuckled. "One of us should change."

"At least we both have good taste," Sophie said.

Esther looked out the big windows that made up the west wall of the library. The trees were bare. The air was cold, and the whole world was gray.

"Necanicum got a case of the winter grays," Esther said.

"If you don't like the weather, wait five minutes. That's what the locals tell me," Sophie said.

"Pretty sure you're a local after all these years."

"Not."

"I just wish the fog in my brain would clear," Esther said. "We know Stanley is on an account that Alvah is taking money from. We know there is a long-standing criminal connection between Alvah and Draven. What we don't know is how Ash fits in. They didn't meet in prison because Ash was in prison in Utah."

"Good grief, Charlie Brown. Is everyone a criminal or serial killer?"

Esther chuckled. "Only in Necanicum and St. Mary Mead."

"Miss Marple was a serious murder magnet."

"Right? I am still going to ask my dad about Ash. Maybe they knew each other."

"We also need to talk to Kol. If we go to Sandy Stories early, maybe we can catch up to him," Sophie said.

Esther stopped and looked at her, one brow raised. "And what? Ask him? Hey, Kol, did you try to kill Stanley? We saw you with the can collector. He took money from Alvah. Was that a payoff for removing the bolts from the shelves and taking the book?"

"Now that you put it like that..." Sophie grinned sheepishly and shrugged.

"Have you seen Kol? He has perma angry face. I expect him to explode every time I talk to him."

They stood silently for a moment, each pondering the problem.

"Did he drop out?" Esther asked.

"I don't know. Maybe he does packets."

"You know. There is one more person I should have googled last night," Esther said.

"Who's that?" Sophie asked.

"Ramona."

"You don't seriously think she would hurt Stanley? Her own brother? She doesn't strike me as that evil."

Esther adjusted her backpack. "You're the one that told me serial killers are usually nice neighbors. I'm going to see if I can use the library computer and do a quick search."

"I'll help after I finish up in AP Chemistry."

They walked the three last steps to the door and pushed it open. Esther immediately felt all the anxiety she had melt away. The dark paneled room was filled with books and had a fireplace to read by. In Esther's mind, it felt like the sanctuary she had always craved before they moved to Necanicum.

Ms. Priest sat on one of three overstuffed leather couches. Her lean frame looked tiny against the black leather. She held a steaming cup of tea and was in deep conversation with Madison, who looked up at the girls and smiled.

"Girls. I was just updating Ms. Priest. She has some good thoughts. She also wants to contribute to our Secret Santa project. Have a seat. I brought you hot chocolate."

"Where's Bridget?" Esther asked.

"She had to go to the office and work her first period hours, manning the front as usual. She already has her drink."

Esther loved the feel of the warm cup in her cold hands. "Sophie and I did some digging last night. Did Bridget bring you up to speed about Draven really being Raven and his history with Alvah?"

"Yes. She shared it all with me and Ms. Priest, including the name of your new Bacon Gang. I think you need Bacon Gang T-shirts." She winked at Esther, who tried to wink back. One day Esther would finally learn how to wink, but for now all she could manage was rapid blinking and light laughter.

"I've had another thought. I want to look at Ramona's online history and see if she was linked with Alvah and Draven before they came to Necanicum."

Madison's eyes opened wide, and she leaned forward. "You don't think Ramona would do something like that to her brother, and with Alvah and Draven's help?"

Esther nodded. She didn't want to think Ramona could be the killer. "I love Ramona. I don't want to believe she is capable of hurting Stanley. But to be honest, she could have done it. If she did, she knocked out her competition when Hazel passed. She gained a box of valuable supplies for forgery at garage sale prices, and perhaps didn't mean to hurt Stanley. Maybe she wanted to make herself look like a victim to take the heat off of her."

Madison fell back into the couch. She was frozen, staring off into space, thinking like an author.

"I also want to talk to Kol and Ash about Alvah and the money," Esther said.

"That sounds too dangerous," Madison said.

Esther didn't say anything back to Madison because her mind was made up. She looked at her boots and tried to change the subject.

Madison leaned forward. "The puzzle pieces are coming together. But we are still missing one. Alvah worked at the bookstore and could have sabotaged the banister and pushed Hazel." Madison put her cup down and looked at Esther. "But she couldn't have loosened the bolts or pushed the shelves over since she has an alibi for the time the shelves fell."

"Biscuits. Her alibi is weak. Draven is her alibi and whatever they were doing, they weren't repairing her toilet," Sophie said.

Ms. Priest's brows rose at the suggestion there was something between Alvah and Draven. She took a sip of her tea and said, "The bolts could have been removed hours before the shelves fell. Kol or Ash could have pushed the shelves over for her."

"Ash was with Nephi, but he could have loosened the bolts. See, I keep going round and round. We've got to talk to Kol and Ash. Who knows, maybe they'll rat out Alvah when they know we saw her offer the can man money and talk to Ash at his house," Esther said.

"You'd be playing a dangerous game," Madison said.

"It's not a game. Hazel's death deserves to be treated with more respect."

The first bell rang, and Sophie stood. "I need to get to class. Before I go, it just occurred to me, if someone tried to hurt Stanley once, they might try again."

Bridget came into the library as Sophie went out. "You're never going to guess who must have come into some money."

"Don't make us guess, dear," Madison said.

She plopped down next to her mother. "Raini just came in the office and changed her address from the trailer park across the road to a condo they rented next to the hospital. If she is the only person working and her mother is bedridden, where did the money come from?"

23

— ◆ —

E sther and Sophie made it to the store early. Kol was still dusting shelves, and Raini was unboxing new books behind the counter. The fire was lit, Christmas music played softly, and the trees sparkled. Alvah sat by the fire, sipping tea as Esther and Sophie passed through the store and headed down the hallway toward the kitchen.

"I love how peaceful the store is," Esther said.

"You'd never know it was a hot bed of intrigue and murder." Sophie opened the kitchen door.

Ramona was washing dishes, and Stanley was flipping through channels.

"How are you, Stanley?" Esther asked.

"I've watched all The Andy Griffith Shows. I'm looking for something else to watch." He kept clicking.

"Let me introduce you to a wonderful series," Sophie said.

"Sure." He grinned and handed Sophie the remote. Esther realized that there was no guile in his sparkling eyes.

Sophie took the remote, and in a minute, season one of *Miss Marple* was playing.

"Excellent choice." Ramona dried her hands and smiled at the girls.

Draven Kane burst into the kitchen like a black cloud. He went over to Stanley's bed and leaned into Stanley's face. "You are going to get exactly what you deserve. The chief is onto you."

He nearly spilled Stanley's drink, but Stanley caught the teacup before it went over. Liquid splashed onto Draven's shirt.

"What is going on?" Ramona asked. "What are you talking about—?"

Draven cut her off. "Ramona. Outside." He opened the back door and held it, scowling at her.

Ramona frowned at him. "Excuse me?"

He glowered at her and pointed outside. Ramona looked at the girls and Stanley, shook her head, and then dried her hands and followed him through the back door.

Stanley shook his head. "He shouldn't be like that."

The door slammed shut, rattling the glass in the door's window. Esther couldn't help it. She all but put her ear to the door. She stood to the side of the door, in the shadows, but watched Draven.

"Biscuits. I can't believe she ever saw anything in him," Sophie said.

"Shush," Esther whispered.

The hallway door to the kitchen opened. Kol and Raini came into the kitchen, eyes and mouths wide open.

"What was that?" Raini asked.

"Shush." Esther put her finger to her lips and then pointed out the back door. The television was still running on low, and Stanley seemed to be sleeping through the whole thing.

Ramona was facing the girls, but her arms were folded. Her chin was up, she looked away through angry eyes, and would only give him an occasion glance. She was red with embarrassment and on the verge of raining tears.

It made Esther's heart hurt. Sophie growled softly. Something Draven said struck a nerve with Ramona. She looked at him through narrowed eyes. The thick wood door made it hard for Esther to understand what he was saying.

Then loud enough anyone in the store could have heard, he bellowed, "The police think I tried to hurt Stanley. They are blaming me when Stanley is the one that was robbing you blind. Don't believe his sweet, sappy face. He and Alvah have played us!" He waved his arms, emphasizing the *us*. "Well? What are you going to do about it? You owe me money. My half!"

When money came up, Ramona looked up. All the sadness had burned away. All that was left was rage. "There is no us! Leave now!"

"I'm a part owner!"

"Of some of the books! Not of the store or any other item in the store. I didn't put your name on a single thing I didn't have to. I smelled a skunk the minute you started helping Alvah every day."

Esther heard the bell ringing. Someone was coming into the store.

Draven stepped back, and his body language shifted while Ramona yelled, holding Esther's attention. Hands on his hips, he barked. "I'll sue you! I've invested. Alvah, that woman you hired, is inept. Of course I helped her. She's pathetic, really. I only spent time with her because she appreciated me. It didn't mean anything. You were busy with this store and your brother and sister. A nice woman like you couldn't give me what I wanted."

"Well, whatever it is you want, you're never going to get it from me! I am a nice girl, and proud of it!" Ramona tried to walk past him. He stuck his arm out, stopping her.

With spit flying, he said, "You goody, goody. I hate your pious soul!"

A large hand pulled Esther and Sophie back. Ash Corradao opened the door so fiercely it slammed against the outside wall. The screen door didn't stand a chance. He left it hanging crooked.

"Leave! Go!" Ash's deep voice shook Esther to the center of her soul. His muscular arm pointed away from the house.

All the color left Draven's face. He took a step back like a vampire trying to avoid the stake Ash wanted to pound into his heart. As he stumbled away, he raised a fist. "I told the chief all about Stanley. He's the one! Alvah killed Hazel for Stanley. He loved her!"

Sophie pushed past Ramona, pointing at Draven. "You're a black-hearted, bagel-munching Raven!"

Ash stepped between Ramona, Sophie, and Draven's retreating figure.

"Sophie," Esther hissed, reached out, and tried to pull her back.

Ash stood face to face with Ramona and gently took both her hands in his. "Did he hurt you?"

Ramona shook her head. His kindness burst the dam, and her tears flowed freely. Esther looked down at her feet, wanting to give her some privacy. Sophie tore a paper towel off the roller and handed it to her.

She smiled. "Thanks, Sophie. What did you call him?"

"Sorry. I know I shouldn't swear like that."

Ramona shook her head and chuckled softly.

Nephi ran into the kitchen. "The police are on their way!"

He pulled Esther and Sophie close to his tall frame and held them protectively.

Kol and Raini looked on quietly from the hall.

"Ramona? What do you want me to do? I can talk to the police, or I can go after him," Ash said. The dark energy Draven left behind evaporated with Ash's calm and gentle tone.

"You don't need any more attention from the police," Ramona said. "But thank you for offering to take care of me."

"I mean it."

"I know you do. Go ahead and go back to the bakery. I am sure Bubba and Parker are worried." Ramona smiled, took a deep breath, and exhaled loudly. "I can handle this."

"I am going around the building and making sure he's really gone," Ash said. "When you're ready, we need to talk, but not right now. You've been through enough."

"Okay. I'll come over after we close."

Ash put a hand on her shoulder and gave it a friendly squeeze before he left her to make sure Draven was truly gone.

Ramona and the girls watched him go.

Esther looked up at Nephi. "Where's Parker?"

"He called the police and is manning the store."

Ramona came back into the kitchen and stood, with her eyes closed, at the sink.

"I've got another call to make." Nephi stepped outside the broken screen door, his back to Esther.

Esther looked at Sophie, whose fists were still clenched. "He's a liar."

"He's something all right," Sophie said.

Kol scowled at her and stood protectively in front of Raini.

Ramona shrugged, turned, and smiled. "Show's over. Hopefully there weren't any customers in the store. Kol, Raini, why don't you clean up and clock out? Sophie and Esther will be out in a minute."

The girls and Ramona waited until the kitchen was empty and Stanley was softly snoring.

"Wow. I can't believe he can sleep through that," Sophie said.

Ramona chuckled and smiled lovingly at Stanley. "He's slept through every church service and major event of his adult life."

"What can we do to help? We can watch the store so you can take a break," Esther said.

"I am so sorry you had to witness that, girls."

Esther shook her head no. "It's not your fault. You have nothing to apologize for. We want to help. We've been trying to help."

"What do you mean?" Ramona asked.

"Helping you lets us keep working in this wonderful place," Sophie said and gave Ramona an insincere smile.

Esther closed her eyes, searching for a way to tell Ramona what they had done and what they knew. "It's just... Draven so obviously cared more for the books and himself than you or anyone else. We saw Stanley looking at some interesting things online before the accident. We also didn't believe Hazel's death was an accident. Since the ink bottles in the box you bought were the same as the bottles Stanley was looking at online, well... we had to know."

"Chief Lampii was here talking to Stanley when we opened this morning. The chief asked for our computers. I think that's why Draven came over and got online," Ramona said.

"Did you give them to the chief?" Esther asked.

Ramona shook her head. "I know enough to know I can ask them to come back with a warrant, unless they have probable cause or it's an emergency. Anyway, they'll probably be back soon with a warrant. The only thing that will slow them down is the holidays. I heard the detective telling the chief she was flying back to Seattle to spend Christmas with family, and she didn't want this to interfere. The chief told her to go. He didn't look so happy with her."

Nephi came back into the kitchen. "I'm going out front to meet the officers."

"Who did you call?" Esther asked. He left quickly without answering.

Ramona looked back and forth between the girls. "Esther, from something you said the other day, I'm guessing you know what's on the computer. Raini tells me you two are some kind of supersleuths."

Esther felt her cheeks burn. She touched them, sure they were on fire and her face was bright red. Esther looked at Sophie.

Sophie caught the unsaid plea for help. "We just find ways to dig ourselves out of trouble that seems to follow us." She relaxed her posture and casually leaned against the table, which slid enough she lost her balance. She stood back up and smiled sheepishly at Esther.

"We do like solving puzzles. In fact, we can't stand it until we have the pieces put together," Esther said.

Ramona exhaled loudly. "Then Draven came by this morning after the chief and got on the computers. I knew something was wrong. At first, he was okay. He even brought a gift for Stanley. Then he went upstairs to work with the rare books. He told me he was on the computer, comparing the books to the inventory, and that some valuable books were still missing.

But the names of the books that he said were missing were new to me. I told him he needed to double check the records."

"Is it possible there are books you've purchased together that you don't remember?" Esther asked.

"We have hundreds of books, but I have a talent for remembering them. I know every book that is up there. I might not be able to make a complete list, but I could come close."

"Do you think he's intentionally coming up with books you don't have in your inventory, or maybe he doesn't have as good a memory?" Esther asked.

"Draven has a separate rare book company in New York. I asked him if it was possible for him to make a mistake or confuse inventory lists. He said no, and I had no reason to doubt him."

"Do you have access to his New York business?" Esther asked.

"No. When I checked our online record, the books were in the inventory. How they got there, I don't know. Technically, our inventory list is what the business insurance will look at when it calculates our losses from the accident."

"Can he access your online systems remotely?" Esther asked.

"In theory. I've never tried it. It's hard enough to live at work, much less carry it around in my pocket on my phone. It's just that Draven wasn't himself. I think he might be the person that called Chief Lampii and the reason the chief is asking questions and wants our computer."

"You need a better fiancé," Sophie said.

"I think I shall go without one for quite a while after this." After sitting down on one of the chairs, Ramona rubbed her face with her hands. Then she looked up. "I was hoping I could ask you girls to get on the computers and figure out what Stanley was doing and if anyone was helping him. I've heard you're a genius with computers, Sophie."

"I am. I am the best I know. You're lucky to get our help before we graduate with our doctorate and can charge what we're worth." Sophie smiled, and Ramona chuckled again.

"Ramona? Sophie and I have something to confess," Esther said. A small foot stepped on hers. She looked down at Sophie, who rolled her eyes and tipped her head.

"She needs to know, Sophie," Esther said.

Sophie's shoulders slumped, and she looked down at her feet, avoiding Ramona and Esther's gaze.

"The other night," Esther said, "after we closed up and you were all up at the hospital, we looked at the computers in the rare books room."

Ramona stared incredulously.

Esther went on. "We'd seen Stanley looking up books, inkwells, and quills online before the accident. Frankly, because of Hazel's death, it sent up some red flags. We wanted to figure out what he might be involved in or doing. We didn't know he was... dyslexic."

Ramona sat quietly, listening, with her hands steepled and pressed against her lips, as if she wanted to speak but her hands were holding in all her words.

"What we found made us concerned that someone might be taking advantage of Stanley and your trust in him," Esther said.

Ramona's hands dropped, and she studied Esther's face through narrowed eyes.

"We started our research with the search history on the computer," Sophie said.

"The search history led us to an online auction house that specializes in rare and valuable books," Esther said.

Sophie held up a finger, like a teacher making a point. "By the way, you must password protect your computer. Anyone could get on it and into your accounts. I'll help you today if you want."

"I would love some help."

"Anyway, after Soph found the site, it opened and populated a saved username and password, which got us past the login. We found Stan's account with more than a hundred thousand dollars in merchandise listed."

"What? Where did he get that kind of money?"

"There's more. Alvah's credit card was being used on the account. That means her account was used to purchase and to receive funds. But it didn't prove that she knew about the use of her credit card," Esther said.

"Alvah." Ramona almost growled when she said Alvah's name. "I let her stay in the tiny house because she lost her job, and now she's manipulating Stanley. It's time we had a little talk."

Ramona got up, crossed the kitchen, and navigated the hall in less than a second. Esther and Sophie followed, but it was hard to keep up with her pace. She sped past the cash register with Esther and Sophie on her heels. Kol was standing at the counter, leaning over, and talking quietly to Raini, who was unboxing new books.

"Alvah," Ramona said.

Alvah was sitting in the wingback chair by the fireplace. A teacup was on the small table by the chair. Her face was hidden by the chair.

"Alvah. We need to talk upstairs in my office right now," Ramona said sternly. She stopped in front of Alvah with her arms folded.

They dropped. Her eyes widened. She covered her opened mouth with her hands and looked at Esther. Ramona looked around the room wildly. Kol and Raini were staring at her.

"Is there anyone else in the store?" Ramona asked.

Raini shook her head no.

"No. Why?" Kol asked.

"Sophie, change the sign to closed. None of you move. I need to check on Stanley." Ramona ran for the kitchen.

Esther moved. She wanted to see Alvah but already knew what she was going to find. Her heart raced so fast she put her hand over it as if she could slow it down. She looked wide eyed at Sophie.

"Alvah is dead," Esther said.

"Shut the front door!" Sophie said.

Alvah was dead. There was no doubt. Her eyes were closed, and her face was peaceful, but Alvah wasn't there anymore.

Even though Parker had called the police and Nephi had announced that they were on their way, Esther dialed nine-one-one.

She put her phone on speaker so Sophie could hear. "Hello? This is Sandy Stories. Can you send an officer? One of the employees has died."

"This is Esther, isn't it? They're on their way. We had a call a few minutes ago. Your stepdad heard. He should be there any minute," Reva, the oldest dispatcher, said. *That must have been who Nephi called, Papa J.* Reva continued with her gravelly voice, but Esther was having a hard time tracking what she was saying. She was trying to memorize everything about Kol, Raini, and the room."

"Esther. Esther!"

"Yes. Sorry."

"What makes you think she's dead?" Reva asked.

"I wish you had FaceTime. Trust me, she's dead."

"I'll check her pulse." Sophie put her hands on Alvah's limp wrist, which was drooped over the arm of the chair. "Yup. Dead as a doornail. What does dead as a doornail even mean?"

Ramona burst into the room. "Get an ambulance! Stanley won't wake up!"

Esther passed Ramona, who followed her as she ran down the hall. Stanley looked gray, sick. His teacup was shattered on the floor. "We need an ambulance too! Stanley Brocklehurst has been poisoned," she told Reva.

"An ambulance and officers are on the way. Could he have overdosed?" Reva asked.

"What?" Esther cried out incredulously.

"Could he have used a prescription or illegal substance?" Reva asked.

"No! He isn't like that," Ramona said. "Stanley, wake up. Stanley!" She vigorously rubbed his hand on the arm without the cast. She tried to pull him up to a sitting position. Esther put down the phone and went to the other side of the bed to help.

Sirens sounded in the distance, growing closer.

"I'll bring them to the kitchen." Sophie ran out the door.

Ash charged into the room and pushed Esther aside. "What happened?" he said over the sirens.

"I don't know. He won't wake up, and Alvah's dead!" Ramona wailed. Ash went to her side and held her when it looked as though her knees might buckle.

24

— • —

E sther held Parker's hand and leaned against Nephi. Bubba and Sophie sat on the porch step watching Ash and a police officer help Ramona climb into the back of the ambulance to ride with Stanley.

Raini and Kol joined them on the porch.

"See you tomorrow, I hope," Raini said.

"If they open the store," Sophie said.

Raini's sweet smile fell.

Kol took her hand, "Come on. Let's get you home." They walked toward town while the group watched.

"Did anyone call Stanley's sister, Principal Brocklehurst?" Esther asked.

Another police car pulled into the parking lot.

"Nope. I called someone else," Nephi said.

Esther groaned.

Parker kissed the top of her head. "Now, now. Let him love you."

She looked up into his beautiful eyes and smiled.

Papa J trotted up the stairs, put his arms around Esther and Nephi. He held them tightly for a full minute before he stepped back, looked at Esther, and shook his head.

"Your mother and Chief Lampii are on the way," Papa J said.

"I don't know who to be more afraid of," Esther said.

Sophie laughed.

"I called your parents too, Sophie. And yes, Parker, I called your dad."

Bubba looked on quietly, alone.

The chief's SUV pulled into the parking lot and practically slid to a stop. He got out and slammed his car door, pulled up and adjusted his duty belt, and his aviators, before he marched toward the silent group. Esther realized Kol was sitting in the back of the Police SUV with Raini.

"What in the name of Jiminy Christmas is going on, Esther?" the chief bellowed.

All six feet four inches of Ash stood up. "Hey now, why are you asking the little girl. I'm here, ask me."

"Because this little girl is always wherever there is murder and mayhem!" the chief barked, spit flying.

They all looked at Esther.

"Speak it sister," Sophie said.

"Chief, I think I know who killed Alvah, Hazel, and is trying to kill Stanley. I can tell you where to find the evidence, but there are still two pieces missing." Esther turned to Ash. "Why did Alvah try to give you money?"

The color drained from Ash's face. He didn't say a word.

"Well?" the chief asked quietly, like a rattle snake waiting for its prey.

Ash's hands fell to his sides. He kicked at something invisible on the floor. "She said she had a job she wanted me to do for cash. A lot of it. I told her no. It's not the first time I have turned her down."

"Give me some answers. I will not be deprived of Christmas dinner because I've got this mess hanging over my head!" the chief exclaimed.

Esther felt Parker's hand squeeze hers tighter and realized he was frowning at the chief.

Papa J took a step toward Ash, who looked down at his feet. He spoke gently. "Ash. It's time we got to the bottom of this. Just what exactly, in detail, was she asking you to do?"

Ash didn't look up. He held his fist up, staring at his hand. "She never said. I didn't let her get that far. I have all the money I need. It didn't matter what she wanted. I wasn't going back to prison for her or anyone else."

"Well, that is not helping your case at all, mister," the chief said.

Esther let go of Parker's hand, walked to Ash, and lightly touched his arm. "Ash? Where did your money come from?"

Ash fell back into the porch swing and slowly looked Esther in the eyes.

"Speak up, young man," the chief said.

Ash looked back down. "I've promised to keep it a secret."

The chief pulled his aviators off and pointed them at Ash. "This is a murder investigation, possibly a double homicide! You had better tell me, or I am going to stop being patient and drive you back to prison myself! It will be my first Christmas gift. I'm recording our conversation." He placed his cell down, with the recording app activated.

Ash looked from the chief to Esther. His hands were shaking.

"Okay. But understand that nothing will change after I tell you unless I go back to prison. I am going to continue to live where I do and run Literal Buns."

"Well now, that depends on what you tell us, doesn't it?" the chief said.

Ash took a deep breath and held out his hand. "Do you see this?"

"The number nine? Are you a member of some sort of cult? The Nine Gang. Is that where your cash flow comes from?" the chief asked.

Ash shook his head.

"Say it for the recording."

"No. I didn't get my money from a gang."

"Who gave it to you?" The chief's face was still red, and Esther could feel whatever patience he had drain away.

"Morgan David Day, Esther's father, gave me the money."

"Shut the front door!" Sophie exclaimed.

Esther gasped. Blood rushed in her ears. She looked at Sophie, who looked back, mouth open, eyes wide.

The chief was speechless.

Ash traced the number nine. "Step number nine. Make direct amends to such people wherever possible, except when to do so would injure them or others."

The chief took his hat off and scratched his head. "I've heard of AA. What has that got to do with the money? Did Esther's father wrong you and give you the money to make amends?"

"No. I wronged others. My addiction to alcohol killed someone. Esther's father was in my AA group in prison. We became friends. He knew I wanted to make amends, and I would be out long before he was. That's why I'm here."

Ash looked at the chief, Papa J, and Esther one by one. "I agreed to do something in secret."

"Did he want you to kidnap her again?" Sophie asked.

A slow smile spread on Ash's face. "Sophie, you're the best friend a kid could ever ask for. No, he didn't ask me to kidnap her." Ash's smile vanished, and he looked straight at Esther. "Esther's dad gave me enough money to come to Necanicum and keep an eye on his baby girl."

Esther's head jerked back. Her brows knit, but he didn't look away.

"Your dad asked for my help after the last time you two were almost killed trying to solve a murder and save your friends. He felt like you needed a bodyguard."

Esther's mind was reeling. She held up a hand as if to stop him from talking. "He doesn't think I can take care of myself?" She opened her eyes and waited.

Ash chuckled and leaned forward, shaking his head and clasping his hands, elbows on his knees. "That's exactly the reason he wanted me to keep everything a secret, and now I've broken his trust to save myself. He said you wouldn't want any help from him. In fact, he thought if you knew he sent me, you might never speak to him again. He knows he deserves to be cut out of your life."

Leaning back against the swing, he looked at Esther, unseeing. "Believe me when I say your dad has remorse." He half smiled. "He's still a hot head, but he's trying, and you're his inspiration. He wants to be there for you. He didn't even want you to know. All he cared about was keeping you safe. And now, I've failed and probably am going back to prison."

"But... Wait... I don't understand. He is in prison. Where did he get that kind of money?" Esther asked.

"You've come this far. You might as well clear the air. I would do it before Officer Hart and Nephi give you what you've got coming," the chief said.

"You have an Uncle, Esther. And you had a grandfather."

"I know. Nephi and Grandpa James. Wait..." The pieces all fell into place. Esther stared off into space, thoughts coming together like a puzzle, and then she realized who he was talking about.

"You're talking about my father's father."

Ash nodded.

"Sophie and I found him online."

"Do you also know your grandfather had a lot of money?" Ash asked.

"I could tell he did by the obituary."

Ash smiled. "The obituary is an understatement. The fact is, he left the son he didn't like three million. That would be your dad. Your uncle advanced your dad enough money to pay me to be a bodyguard, or to at least keep an eye on you and try to keep you safe until he was out."

"Holy guacamole... But how is that making amends? You were paid," Sophie said.

"The amends come from having to leave my old life entirely behind, everything and everyone I knew. I left New York to go to prison in Utah. Now, all I want to do is what I promised and start fresh in Necanicum. I had no idea how beautiful this place would be or that there would be people like Ramona and your Grandma Mable, who could know my past and still accept me."

"We're back to square one," the chief said. "What do you think happened here?" He looked back and forth between Esther and Sophie.

"I got this." Sophie cleared her throat. "Draven Kane is a killer."

"I can believe that. But what happened that makes you so sure?"

Esther raised her hand like a schoolgirl, and the chief nodded. "This all started long before the box Hazel found that led to her death. Draven and Alvah were playing the long con, if that's what it's called. They were also in prison together in Ohio ten years ago. There is evidence that they have been running the same scam in various locations for years.

"I believe they find aged ink and use aged paper from blank or back pages in antique books to create rare documents or signed books. They sell them privately. They could potentially make hundreds of thousands of dollars. They used Ramona to legitimize their business. Stanley was the perfect patsy for their ploy. Alvah would buy the books, the ink, and all the necessary supplies to make the documents using an account in Stanley's name.

"I don't believe Stanley or Ramona knew anything about it. I don't know what Hazel knew or saw that made her a target. But they got away with pushing Hazel through the railing while she and Alvah were unboxing books they bought at auction."

The chief took off his sunglasses and rubbed his eyes. "Do you have proof?"

"Sort of," Esther said. "Not about Hazel, but with Stanley's accident it makes sense. You see, my guess is that Stanley asked about an online auction account with his name on it or did something that made them nervous, so they tried to kill him. When that didn't work, they tried to set him up or make it look like he was stealing books so he would go to jail and be out of the way. That way, they could still use his account or avoid getting caught. They didn't respect Stanley, and they underestimated Ramona's love for Stanley."

The chief ran his fingers through his gray hair, making it stick up. "If they were in it together, why would Draven kill Alvah?"

"To protect himself. We're probably just skimming the surface, but so far, all the financial transactions we found were in Alvah's name or Stanley's. The bank account is hers. Draven would be able to make it look like her idea. The money in her account would be another reason for you or the police to find her guilty of the crimes, including killing Hazel. I think that's why he came over earlier today. He was making sure the money was moved to another account, someplace he could get to it. I also think he was setting himself up to get a fat check from the insurance company, knowing that if she were dead, he wouldn't have to split it with her."

"What killed her?" the chief asked.

"Poison of some kind. Whatever it is, it will be in the tea in her cup and in the tea on Stanley's broken cup," Esther said.

"I'm going to need you girls to type this all up and make a statement explaining how you know everything, before Christmas."

"Oh, biscuits!" Sophie folded her arms, frowning.

"Don't you go complaining, Sophie Ito. This whole thing made a mess of my Christmas. I haven't even bought the missus a gift."

"There is one more thing, Chief," Esther said.

"Get it all out," the chief said.

Esther looked over at Kol in the car. "Kol and a man that collects cans, and I think is his father, took money from Alvah for something."

The entire group turned to stare at Kol.

The chief marched down the stairs, opened the driver's door, and rolled Kol's window down part way.

"Young man, did you take money from Alvah?"

Kol's eyes narrowed. He frowned.

"You better let me know what you took that money for, or you and Raini will be going to the station and getting booked right along with Draven Kane."

Kol deflated. He looked back at Raini and then at the chief. "She wanted my dad to buy liquid Fentanyl for her, or powdered. She didn't care which."

"Did you buy it for her?"

"I didn't, and my dad said we didn't have to. She gave us the money. What was she going to do, complain that we didn't buy her drugs and owed her money? The money was ours," Kol said.

"Do you know anything else about all of this?

"No, sir."

"Then get out of the car, Kol! You and I will have a little chat later. I'm going to need the backseat for Draven Kane." The chief opened the SUV's door. Kol and Raini quickly got out.

"Now we know what probably killed her. I bet Alvah bought the Fentanyl from someone else. She gave it to Draven for Stanley, and Draven put it into her tea as well as Stanley's." Esther said.

"Kol could have put it into her tea," the chief said.

"I believe him. I don't think he did it."

"Why would you believe him?"

"Just a feeling," Esther said. "One I am learning to trust."

"Esther is a highly intuitive empath," Sophie said.

"What did you call her?" Papa J laughed. A black SUV pulled into the parking lot.

"Grandfather?" Parker asked. His brows rose, and he looked at Esther and shrugged.

The tinted window rolled down, and Grandma Mable leaned out, waving. Lord Stuart was smiling and waving at Parker from the passenger's seat. The chief crossed the parking lot to the car.

"Now what did she do?" Grandma Mable asked.

The chief looked at Esther and then back at Grandma Mable and rubbed the back of his neck. "Nothing."

"Then why not let her go, Chief? Lord Stuart and I have plans for these kids. We've got cookies to bake." Then she looked up at Ash. "Ash, are you in? Let's bake something. You too, kids!" She pointed at Bubba.

Bubba grimaced and wrapped his coat tighter around his thin body. "I have to get home. Mom has a night shift, and I have to watch the kids."

"Me and Raini are going with Bubba," Kol said.

"I actually have to get home too," Raini said.

"Hop in. We'll take you home, won't we, Stewie?" Grandma Mable smiled at Lord Stuart.

"Sounds lovely," Lord Stuart said.

25

— • —

E sther looked around the kitchen in amazement. Christmas music was playing in the living room and floating into the kitchen. The fire was lit. Parker was laughing with his grandfather, who had an apron on over a bright red sweater. They were covered in flour and rolling out cookie dough. Paisley and Nephi were decorating the cookies as fast as Esther and Sophie could cut and bake them. Mary was supervising sprinkles.

The family cocker spaniel, Lady, was licking up everything that hit the floor, and Miss Molly was snuggled in her basket by the fire.

Papa J and her mother were having a quiet conversation with Ash in the living room. Esther wanted to know what they were saying, but the sounds of her mother's favorite Christmas playlist, Coffee House Hip Christmas, made it impossible to eavesdrop.

Once she had tried sliding closer to the door. Her mother caught her and wagged a finger in her direction.

The doorbell rang, and Sophie's parents and Parker's parents came in. Sophie and Parker gave each other worried looks.

Sophie leaned close to Esther. "Holy guacamole. What is going on out there?"

Esther grinned. "I can't hear them over all the noise. I did hear Papa J say that they caught Draven trying to leave town and are holding him for questioning."

"I heard." Sophie said. "Way to solve a mystery."

"I'm going to find out." Parker wiped his hands on his apron as if he was going to leave.

"Young man, you most certainly are not," Lord Stuart said. "It isn't polite to interrupt adult conversation or to leave your grandfather alone with a redhead and a rolling pin."

Parker laughed loudly.

"What are you afraid of, Stewie?" Grandma Mable winked at Parker's grandfather, who laughed.

"He giggles like a seven-year-old," Sophie said.

⬥⬥⬥⬥⬥⬥ ⬥⬥⬥⬥⬥⬥

Foil-covered paper plates with red ribbons covered the kitchen table. The sink was full of dishes, but everyone had washed the flour from their hands.

"Are we ready?" Grandma Mable asked.

"What are we doing?" Parker asked.

Mable took charge by stepping up onto the fireplace hearth and motioning for everyone to stop talking. "We are starting a new tradition. You'll have to drive your van so our convoy isn't too large. The grownups will drive two cars. You kids load the plates into the back of Lord Stewie's SUV. Esther, here is a list of where we are going. You give Parker directions and try not to get too far behind."

Lord Stuart helped Grandma Mable down.

"Wait here." She went into the living room and turned off the music. "Alright, all you mature adults, it's time to make a new Christmas memory. Get your warm coats on and get in the SUV!"

Ash got up and walked to the door.

"Oh no you don't. You're riding with my daughter, Grace." Mable handed Esther's mother the same list she gave Esther. "Don't get lost. Okay, let's load 'em up!"

The first stop was the local hospital on the hill. They gathered outside the intensive care unit on the lawn.

"Lord Stewie, in America, we call this Christmas caroling. Let's start with 'Silent Night,'" Mable said.

"Splendid!" He grinned.

"Follow me." Mable raised her arms like a conductor and sang the very first off-key note until everyone joined in. The winter night was dark, but the sky was crystal clear. The lights inside the hospital let Esther see into the patient's rooms. As they sang, she saw Ramona and Principal Brocklehurst wave from a top-floor window.

When the song ended, Grandma Mable gave Esther a plate of cookies. "Why don't you kids give that to the nurses and have it delivered to Stanley's room."

"Can I eat one?" Sophie asked.

"No, Sophie. You will get something to eat. I promise," Grandma Mable said.

Parker, Nephi, Paisley, Esther, Sophie, and Mary walked into the lobby of the hospital. A receptionist sat behind a plexiglass window.

"Are you the cute kids that were singing?" she asked.

"Can you deliver this to Mr. Brocklehurst's room?" Esther asked.

"Sure thing, but he says he isn't hungry yet," she said.

"He's awake?" Esther asked.

"I'm sorry, I can't answer that. It's confidential. But I will happily deliver this plate." She smiled.

The next stop was a neat and tidy cottage nestled in pines on the mountain side. The group began singing "The Twelve Days of Christmas." Ms. Priest opened the door, letting light spill out. She clasped her hands together and bounced on her toes.

"I love Christmas carols. Wait, let me get you something." Ms. Priest closed the door and was back shortly with enough candy canes for the group.

After they delivered cookies to Papa J's friend, Officer Ironpot; the chief; and the station, they had only two stops left.

The first was to Bubba's trailer, where they took four plates to the door for Bubba and his nine brothers and sisters. They sang, "O Come All Ye Faithful." Nine little heads stared out the window. Bubba came out with a baby wrapped in a warm blanket.

At first, he looked confused; then a smile spread across his face. Everyone in the trailer squealed when they were given four paper plates of cookies.

Bubba smiled broadly. "Thanks for the sugar, guys!" His laughter let Esther know he didn't mind the sugar at all and neither did the squealing kids.

Bubba went back inside, where Esther heard him say, "Now leave some of that for Christmas, okay?"

Warmth spread all through her body. She couldn't remember a time when she had felt such peace and joy.

Parker hugged her. "Where to next?"

They drove past the cove and up the mountain to a house only a few blocks away from the Captain's Cove Mansion that Parker and Paisley lived in.

There was another smaller but fascinating home. The walls were large stones. The door was heavy wood with black metal and rounded at the top. A Christmas tree filled the front window.

When they started singing, "Do you hear what I hear?" Madison Merriweather and Bridget came to the door.

"Can we join them, Mom?" Bridget asked.

"Do you have room for two more?" Madison asked.

"There is always room for more fun," Grandma Mable said.

The last stop was the large home that sat next to Esther's home. The group sang, "We wish you a Merry Christmas," until Marion and two of his cats joined them on the porch. Another cat slept in his window.

"Anne Freid! Get out of the Christmas tree," Marion said.

"Do you guys want to stay up and watch movies?" Nephi asked.

"Do chickens have delicious legs?" Sophie asked.

"Oh no you don't. It is the night before the night before Christmas. I am not going to wake up to a sea of buttered popcorn on the floor," Esther's mother said.

"Can I sleep over?" Sophie asked.

"No. You sneak in the window like you always have." Grandma Mable cackled.

Sophie's parents looked over their glasses at Sophie. "You're spending Christmas Eve and Christmas in your own bed. Besides, Spam would miss you."

"Who is Spam?" Lord Stuart asked.

"He's our Shih Tzu," Sophie said.

"Gesundheit," Lord Stuart said. He and Grandma Mable snickered together, smiling at each other joyously.

As everyone was leaving, Esther stopped Ash on the front porch. "Can you come over tomorrow morning at eight?"

"Why?"

"Trust me," Esther said.

"I have issues with trust."

"Me too."

26

— • —

The sky outside Esther's window was salmon pink and blue with wispy clouds at eight a.m. Christmas Eve morning. The ocean was loud enough that she could clearly hear the rhythmic waves crashing on the sandy shore. The sun was just peeking over the eastern mountains. She slept with her window open, even in December. The sound of the ocean and fresh breeze were like a lullaby to her. A small gust of wind made her curtains dance.

She wanted to put on her running shoes and run the sea wall, but she had an obligation.

She slipped on her white hoodie, jeans, and knit boots. She gathered her laptop, charger, and phone as back up and softly padded down the stairs. Even though the sun was growing brighter, she plugged in the Christmas tree and set the laptop up on the coffee table.

There was a soft rap on the door. She pulled it open and let Ash in.

"Nice shoes," Ash said.

"You're being sarcastic, right?"

"No. I actually hate cold feet, and they look warm." He gave her a rare smile.

"We have to hurry."

Ash sat across the room while she sat on the sofa, set up the laptop, and joined the video call with her father.

"Esther. I got your gift." Her dad's scarred face gave her a crooked half smile.

Esther's heart warmed, surprising her. "Hi, Dad."

He smiled broader, pulling his scar tight. "My therapist is here."

Esther just nodded.

"She's off screen. She just wanted you to know this is being recorded as part of my therapy."

A box popped up, and she had to check that she approved the recording.

"Dad? Open your package."

"Shouldn't I wait for Christmas? It's my only package."

"Please."

He used his mangled hands and tore the brown wrapping paper. He opened it to reveal a scrapbook. His face snapped up. Shocked, he let out a surprising sob. He looked back down and ran his hand over the cover.

In a voice choked with tears, he said. "I... I..." He wiped his eye with the back of his hand.

"Open it, Dad."

"The Good Times by Esther James." The picture on the front of the book was of her father, a young, handsome man, holding his baby girl in his arms for the first time.

He carefully opened the album and unstoppable tears flowed. Page after page of all the good times. The time he taught her to ride a bike, tie her shoes, his smiling face next to hers while she put her entire face into her first birthday cake. Esther's favorite photo of her father in a tube, behind a boat, holding Esther in his lap, laughing together, eyes lit up with joyful glee.

Her first day of kindergarten, holding his hand as they walked away from home, Esther wearing her little plaid backpack.

The last photo was of a Christmas tree. Their last Christmas together. She was holding a doll almost as big as she was. He was putting training wheels on her new bike.

A tear ran down her cheek, surprising her. She realized she had been holding her breath.

"This... Thank you." His smile made her laugh. She cried. He cried. No words were spoken. Tears, laughter, and a new feeling, a lightness that comes from forgiving. She felt Joy.

"I..." Someone off screen handed him a tissue. He shook his head and covered his eyes with it. He took in a shaky deep breath and tried to talk again.

"I set this meeting up because it's time for step nine, and I could only think of one thing to give you," he said.

"Dad. I don't need anything..." She pulled her hands inside her sleeves and used one to wipe her eyes.

He held a hand up. "Wait. This isn't about things. This is about... about... You mean so much to me, Esther. I don't want to give you anything; I want to give you everything. Everything I have and am, and it still isn't enough to fill the empty places and pain I've caused us both."

"Dad. It's okay. It all brought me to this place." She held her hands out. "I have so much, Dad. Look at all the good things that came out of the bad things, including this call. They're priceless to me."

A sob wrenched from deep in his chest. He took in a shaky breath and blew it out slowly.

She smiled through her tears and waited while he tried to calm down.

"I have one more gift," Esther said.

His brows knit in confusion, but he had no words.

She motioned for Ash to come over. She made room for him on the couch. They put their heads together and looked into the camera at a man who was so overcome with joy there wasn't anything he could say if he could have spoken.

Someone off screen handed him a water bottle. He wiped his eyes and took a sip, trying to compose himself.

"My friend," Esther's father said. "You aren't very good at keeping secrets, are you?"

Ash's deep chuckle made Esther laugh with him. "I'm pretty good at mysteries, Dad, but you got me on this one."

He shook his head. Someone in the background spoke softly. Her dad nodded in that person's direction, took a deep breath, and blew it out slowly, shaking.

"Esther, I want you to know that I am entirely responsible for the mistakes I have made that destroyed our family and harmed you. There is nothing in this world that will replace those lost years for me or you. But in an effort to make amends to you, I am sending my brother, Mustang, to the house today. It's too late to make peace with my father, but Mustang is anxious to meet you and deliver my gift." Once all his words tumbled out, he took another shaky breath and looked at her, apprehensively.

"Honest, Dad. I have everything I want, including a massive bodyguard."

He beamed. The person in the background spoke a little louder. "I have to go, but I want you to have everything I have. Merry Christmas, baby girl."

"Merry Christmas," Ash said with his deep voice.

"Merry Christmas, Dad."

Esther looked up to see her mom standing at the bottom of the stairs, openly weeping. They embraced and invited Ash into the hug and their family.

27

— · —

P arker and Esther sat under the Christmas tree on Christmas Eve. The house was full of people who loved each other talking, laughing, and feasting on good food, hot wassail, and friendship. Grandma Mable and Lord Stuart were running the music and talking softly by the fire.

"Open it." Esther put her hands together, waiting to see if he liked her homemade gift.

He beamed and held up a photo album that said, "The Bacon Gang's 1972 VW Van," on the front. She had filled it with pictures of the van before the journey, the day he rolled it into the garage at Esther's house, and the expression Sophie caught on his face the day he came in and Papa J had removed all the windows without warning. Photos of Bridget, Nephi, Paisley, and Sophie helping him endlessly sand the primer before it was painted. Paisley and Bridget sitting on the cold floor of the garage sewing designer seat covers. The last pages were of the van's maiden road trip down the coast. Her mother had taken the last picture. In it, all their surfboards were still on a rack on top of the van, the side door open, and in the background the gang was running for the California ocean.

"No one has ever made anything like this for me before. I will treasure it all my life. All I got you was this dumb bracelet," he said. His smile was as genuine as the tears glistening in his eyes.

He handed her a blue box with a white ribbon tied around it. Inside was a thin gold cuff bracelet with a silver infinity symbol on it.

She put her hand over her mouth. He put it on her wrist.

"Forever. Come what may. You will always be precious to me. I can't imagine feeling this way about another human being on this earth. I love your brains most, your tender heart, and beautiful face, and your wild curls. I love you, Esther James."

Under the Christmas tree, they kissed once.

Snow fell softly outside, landing on the salty sea, and melted like her heart.

28

—·—

The few presents that lay under the tree had all been opened, except for Mary's. Santa had brought Mary a dollhouse with tiny animals that lived in it. He had wrapped every animal, tiny chair, tiny table, and tiny refrigerator separately. With every single package, Mary squealed joyfully and put the new piece into the bright colored house.

The doorbell rang.

"I didn't know the doorbell worked," Grandma Mable said.

"Merry Christmas! I fixed it," Papa J said as he got up off the floor to answer it.

"He's a keeper," Grandma Mable said to Esther's mom.

Esther had climbed up on the soft couch and was just contemplating a seven a.m. nap when a stranger came in.

"Hello, Mustang," Papa J said.

Esther stood and looked into the clearest blue eyes. She had only seen eyes this blue once before in her life, during their first Christmas in Necanicum long, long ago. She put her hands over her mouth but couldn't stop joyful laughter from escaping.

"Hello, Esther," Mustang said. "And is this little Mary?"

"I'm big." Mary continued unwrapping tiny gifts while her mother invited him into the room.

"Esther, Papa J and I agree that you are mature enough to know about this gift. However, we don't think you're mature enough to manage it on your own, so we will be your trustees."

"Trustees?" Esther asked.

Mustang held out a large manilla envelope. She opened it.

Inside, a packet of papers had a cover sheet that said, "Trust Fund."

"Your father is giving you and Mary most of his inheritance," Mustang said. "That leaves you both with a little over a million dollars each. You will receive some now. You may spend some at the discretion of your parents, Joseph Hart and Grace James. I will assist in financial decisions and introduce you to my financial planner."

He went on, but Esther was so overwhelmed the words stopped making sense. And then the idea that had taken root deep in her soul last week overflowed.

"I know what I want to do with this money," Esther said. "I know exactly what to do. How much cash can I get my hands on today?"

The blue eyes drew together in confusion. "It's important to use your assets wisely." He tipped his head and frowned, waiting for her explanation.

"Do you trust me?"

"This is our first meeting."

"I know. Our families voted on something before Christmas, but because of some things that happened at work, it didn't get done. This means we can do what we planned," Esther said.

"I'm still confused. But since your father asked me to give you five thousand dollars spending money for the next year, I brought it in cash."

"Perfect!" Esther exclaimed. "I also need a dependable and safe vehicle. Automatic preferable, but that can wait a week."

One of his eyebrows rose. "How generous of you."

She giggled. "Mary, do you want to have some fun?"

"I'm having fun."

"You can come with the Bacon Gang."

Mary and the Bacon Gang climbed out of Parker's van. Everyone gathered around Esther. As quietly as she could, she gave them directions. "Okay. Follow my lead and be as quiet as possible. Don't get caught. It isn't that safe here."

They followed a small dirt path through trees until they came to a clearing. Papa J slowly drove the old Cherokee into the center of the clearing and ran back to the trees for cover with the kids.

"Your mom is parking at the gate," he whispered.

She nodded. "Okay, Mary, you're up."

"This is fun." Mary took a red box with a bow on it in her tiny hands. She sprinted across the clearing, past the Jeep, and up to Bubba's front door. She set the package down, hammered the door with her tiny fists, and ran back for the woods.

Bubba swung the door open, looking angry. Two small twin girls and a small boy came out.

"A present," one of the twins said.

"Don't touch that." Bubba picked it up warily. He shook it and stared in confusion at the Jeep in the clearing. He untied the ribbon and gave it to one of the twins. He carefully opened the red wrapping paper, folding it as though he might use it again. They gathered around the box in anticipation. He set it down on the porch and lifted the lid off.

"Money!" the little boy squealed. The children jumped up and down in excitement.

Bubba was motionless, holding a key and a paper that had come from the box. He looked around at the tree line and poked his head around the side of the trailer.

Barefoot, he ran across the frozen grass and opened the Jeep door, jumped in, and turned the key.

"Yes! Yes! Yes!" He threw both arms in the air, reckless with joy. "Who wants a ride?" He honked the horn. A thin, tired-looking woman came to the door with a small child on her hip. Her eyes grew wide as she stooped to gather up the cash fluttering to the ground.

After delivering a similar package of money to Raini's new condo, they walked to the end of the world, or the trees at the mouth of the river that flowed into the sea. Her mother, the Stuarts, Itos, Madison, and Marion followed behind the kids.

"Did you hear how Raini and her mom got into the condo?" Nephi asked.

"No. Did you?" Esther asked.

"Kol gave her the money. He said some stupid woman gave it to him." With a smug smile on his face, he winked at her, knowing full well Esther had never mastered the art of winking.

The Bacon Gang and their parents gathered outside the small stand of trees.

"We only need one person to go in. It needs to be someone that they don't know."

"I would be happy to deliver the package," Lord Stuart said.

"Atta boy, Lord Stewie." Mable patted him on the back. "Let's go together."

Lord Stuart took the red package in his hands. "What if his father uses it to buy drugs or alcohol? Wouldn't it be better to get them into a program?"

"This isn't about them or what they do with it," Esther said.

"Come again?" Lord Stuart asked.

"It's about us, about me, about who we are. People were there for Mom and me when we were down, and now it's our turn to be there for someone else."

The End

About the Author:

Shannon Symonds writes in an old house by the sea, where her 6 children, their children, 30 or 40 of her closest relatives, and dogs come and go constantly. She loves laughter, a good mystery, running on the beach, deep sea fishing, and bonfires.

In 2021, 2022 she was awarded the Author Ready Author to Watch Award for her By the Sea Cozy Mystery YA series. Her books can be found at Deseret Book, Barnes & Noble, Costco, and Amazon.

Shannon has worked for over 20 years as an Advocate serving survivors of abuse alongside law enforcement, as a home visitor supporting new mothers, and on other causes that she is ridiculously passionate about. Shannon has been a hybrid author since 2014. She authored 263 articles for Deseret Digital Media under her name and with her daughter, blogs for Hilary Weeks Billion Clicks project, the Operation Underground Railroad's volunteer newsletter between 2017 and 2020, and published her first book with Cedar Fort in 2017. Shannon received the Oregon Trial Lawyers Public Justice Award 2002 for the Tiffany Alvera Case that changed housing for victims nationally, and the 2002 Star Advocate Commendation from the Oregon Department of Justice. In 2020, Shannon was the Operation Underground Railroad Volunteer of the Year for the Authors for Freedom Event and her work organizing a 5k Run to Break to Chain.

She will tell you, "Love really is the answer. It always was, and it always will be." And then she'll tell you a story that will put you on the edge of your seat and leave you laughing. @shannonsymondsauthor

CPSIA information can be obtained
at www.ICGtesting.com
Printed in the USA
LVHW101518131222
735135LV00005B/472

9 781958 626214